Bless
the
Beasts
&
Children

Glendon
Swarthout

POCKET BOOKS

New York   London   Toronto   Sydney   Tokyo   Singapore

This book is a work of fiction. Names, characters, places and incidents are products of the author's imagination or are used fictitiously. Any resemblance to actual events or locales or persons living or dead, is entirely coincidental.

POCKET BOOKS, a division of Simon & Schuster Inc 1230 Avenue of the Americas, New York, NY 10020

Copyright © 1970 by Glendon Swarthout
Introduction copyright © 1995 by Miles Swarthout
Reader's Supplement copyright © 1995 by Pocket Books,
a division of Simon & Schuster Inc.

Published by arrangement with Bantam Doubleday Dell,
Publishing Group, Inc.

ISBN: 0-671-52151-9

First Pocket Books printing April 1995

10 9

POCKET and colophon are registered trademarks of
Simon & Schuster Inc.

Cover design by Jeanne M. Lee
Cover art by Steve Brennan

Printed in the U.S.A.

FOR MILES,
WHO WAS THERE, AND TOLD ME

But where is the boy
Who looks after the sheep?
He's under the haystack,
Fast asleep.
Will you wake him?
No, not I.
For if I do,
He'll be sure to cry.

INTRODUCTION

Bless the Beasts & Children was conceived at the tail end of one of this country's most tumultuous decades, the 1960s, when Americans both young and old were ruthlessly and publicly re-examining our national ideals about war, patriotism, public service and social responsibility. Privately, our social fabric was also starting to tear at the seams. America's traditional nuclear families were under bombardment by radical social philosophers espousing such explosive concepts as open marriage and free love. We faced public protests over virtually every important issue during those chaotic years, from international geopolitics right down to banning books from public school libraries.

Glendon Swarthout's *Bless the Beasts & Children* reflected this social upheaval in America. Glendon once wrote that *Bless the Beasts* was a book "about bedeviled boys and great, ungovernable animals, and no man, I thought, could gentle them to his will. It had two larger themes: that all living things are kin, and that by freeing others, we free ourselves."

As an allegory, the book can be appreciated on many levels as each reader finds within it themes and characters and incidents and behaviors to which he or she can relate. From readers around the world Glendon received more than five hundred letters and phone calls thanking him for writing *Bless the Beasts* and asking questions about its origins and meaning. Glendon, as a college English professor of long standing, tried to answer every one.

One left-handed, red-haired, twenty-year-old adventuress from Franconia College in New Hampshire gave herself the middle name of "Teft" and took off for a summer's jaunt out West, car-camping in her Volkswagen fastback with her boyfriend. She retraced the Bedwetters' entire journey. East of Flagstaff on old Route 66, she located the *real* Raymond Ranch and in a long, stream-of-consciousness narrative to my father reported what happened next.

Then we went down to Flag[staff] and with the help of the book and asking people, found the Buffalo Preserve. Thanks—it was the best place we got to see the whole vacation. . . . We drove all over "the pampas"—parked off the road somewhere and walked so we couldn't see anything but land, and there were the buffalo, down in this gorge. Jesus Christ! I turned my head and looked around—just horizon everywhere and turning kind of pink. So the buffalo heard us and ran in a stream up the side of the gorge, onto a plain. That was the last time I remember having actual fun, running on the rocks just before it got dark, to this kind of bush to hide behind so they wouldn't scare. Rob drew a tree—the trees were strange, bent —but creative me just stood there and felt potential.

And still it continues. I was staying at my mother's house in Scottsdale, Arizona, in late April of 1994, beginning my research for this introduction among my father's papers in the Special Collections branch of the Hayden Library at Arizona State University in Tempe. The phone rang Saturday night and it was a lady schoolteacher in Denver who'd tracked us down through directory assistance. She'd been teaching *Bless the Beasts* for the past two years to her high school English classes and just wanted to say "thank you." I explained who I was and that I'd begun work on this new introduction to the novel's special commemorative edition. Then the dear lady broke down, crying that she'd read the book as a student back when she was having a difficult time in high school herself, and how much this novel had helped and encouraged her then.

I thanked her for her support and for remembering, and then got off the phone and told my mother, Kathryn, how amazing this was. "Not at all," she replied, explaining that she still receives a couple of letters and phone calls nearly every month, all concerning an incredible story that's now twenty-five years old. That teacher's phone call was my first exposure in many years to its fans' fondness for and the depth of feeling engendered by this one novel.

Consequently I thought it might be enlightening to future generations of young readers (and their teachers) to attempt to answer some of the more regularly asked questions about *Bless the Beasts*.

Many students have asked who the "Miles" was in this novel's dedication, and if the line "who was there, and told me" meant that this tale was true.

Miles, of course, is me. I'm the only child of Glendon and Kathryn Swarthout. I attended Hidden Valley Ranch for Boys in Prescott, Arizona, for four summers—two years as a camper when in my mid-teens, then two summers as a counselor. The summer following my freshman year (1965) in college I spent as a camp counselor in charge of a cabinful of twelve-year-olds (the *worst* age for boys!), before finally saying goodbye to Hidden Valley Ranch. So yes, my dad was quite familiar with this particular camp, having visited me numerous times on Parents Day and having listened avidly to my camp stories. Check out Stanley Kramer's movie on videocassette; it was shot right at Hidden Valley Ranch, called Box Canyon Boy's Camp in the novel, although there aren't any box canyons around the Prescott area. Alas, Hidden Valley Ranch is gone now, its valuable acreage sold and turned into a real estate development.

Hidden Valley Ranch was the 320-acre Arizona retreat of Dr. Robert Nichols, a Los Angeles orthopedic surgeon. For eight weeks every summer he leased his ranch out to Jim White, a Tucson high school teacher who organized and ran the camp for profit, and the fees for the two month-long sessions were fairly expensive. It was an all-male operation with no more than fifty boys aged twelve through seventeen in residence at its peak. The big focus was on riding, with two kids assigned to every horse. We rode daily, with bi-weekly rodeo events, culminating in a forty-mile, twelve-hour endurance ride at the end of every summer for the hardiest boys. So the novel's camp slogan, "Send Us a Boy—We'll Send You a Cowboy," was right on the mark.

We also had the usual run of camp activities, but the additional big selling points were the weekly campouts at scenic spots all over northern Arizona —Sunset Crater, the Petrified Forest, Oak Creek Canyon, Flagstaff's San Francisco Peaks. Different groups of boys got to go on trips depending on their ages and the physical difficulty of the trek, but we had a camp truck on the road headed somewhere almost every week.

Yes, quite a bit of the background and incidents in *Bless the Beasts & Children* are true. It *was* competitive among the cabins (named for working cowboy classifications—Top Hands, Wranglers, etc.—not Indian tribes), there was occasional night raiding and the usual juvenile pranks, and the weekly winners of the most points—for cleanest cabin and sporting contests—*did* get to go to a movie in town. But cabins were arranged according to the boys' ages; there was no Bedwetters' grouping of oddballs nobody else wanted to bunk with. Stuffed game animals' heads *were* hung around the dining hall, which is where Dad got that bit of business. Like me, a number of the campers were Arizona-bred, their folks sending them out of Phoenix's and Tucson's blazing summer heat up to Prescott, which is the higher-elevated, cooler, summer camping area of Arizona.

Hidden Valley Ranch also took in a number of young dudes from the wealthier environs of Chicago and New York, signed up by camp recruiters working their ritzy suburbs. Overprivileged and overprotected in some instances, as described in the novel, their wealthy, loving (in most cases) parents wanted their offspring to see some scenery and to get toughened up a little, some of the big-city sass knocked out of them. Hidden Valley Ranch was *never* a bootcamp for "bad seeds," though. Rather, it functioned more like the Boy and Girl Scouts have always done, or the more rugged

Outward Bound programs do today, teaching teen-agers outdoor skills and an appreciation of nature, boosting self-confidence and self-reliance in boys and helping them grow up in a fun rough-and-tumble environment.

I will never forget, though, one brutal hike into the Grand Canyon during my summer as a junior counselor. A group of us had hiked down the Bright Angel Trail to spend two nights and a layover day at the Phantom Ranch campground. The third day we hiked back out, taking the shorter but much steeper Kaibab Trail, a steep, grueling eight-mile climb back up to the South Rim. It was hot and two-thirds of the way up we ran out of water. The camp activities' director who led us decided to take the last of the filled canteens with him so that he and another counselor could hurry out, drive our camp trucks back to our parking lot and bring some water back down to the rest of us if necessary. As the strongest of the two remaining counselors, I was charged with herding the stragglers in the rear. Burdened like a donkey with these kids' cameras, empty canteens, bedrolls and cooking gear, I did so. Still emblazoned in my memory is the scream-ing tantrum thrown by one of the young scions of a wealthy Chicago family, who refused to hike one step farther. *His* father could afford to buy the mules to come down and get him, *his* father could rent the helicopter needed to fly in to rescue us all!

Exhausted and parched, I finally got fed up with arguing and walked farther up a switchback, out of sight, to wait for him. Finally cried out and afraid of being left behind, the young tycoon-to-be trudged on and eventually staggered out of the Grand Canyon under his own power. This near-deadly hike resulted in heat prostration among several of the boys and counselors, however, and was one of the two most dangerous situations I was ever involved in while summering at Hidden Valley Ranch. Glendon combined that experience and a rainy midnight march out of Havasupai Canyon (a tributary of the Grand, famed for its stunning waterfalls and river pools in which you can swim), when we were forced to hike out in the dark due to the sudden flash flooding of its creek, to create the flashback near the novel's end, when the Bedwetters endure a forced march out of Havasupai Canyon in order to win a bet Cotton makes with the senior boys.

Let's just say that like all good artists, my father used many of the factual events and details I told him and then took creative liberties with the truth.

Readers are often confused as to the origins of the novel's title, whether *Bless the Beasts & Children* was taken from the Bible.

Actually, this title was not taken from any biblical or literary source, but it *was* divinely inspired!

As my mother told me, *Bless the Beasts* was originally titled *The Bedwetters* before Glendon realized that one wouldn't work and changed it to something else which, unfortunately, she's forgotten. After she and my father went to air-freight the manuscript off to his publisher, Glendon was walking back to the car when he suddenly said, "Well . . . bless the beasts and the children." He then clapped his hands in delight and said, "That's it! That's my title!" The next day he had his New York agent type up a new title page and send it over to Doubleday.

It certainly became a famous title, as well as a hit theme song for the Carpenters and Andy Williams. Who knows where or when or how inspiration will strike—you just have to be open to it. But all us Swarthouts sure like this anecdote!

Bless the Beasts & Children was inspired by an incident that happened in my own restless youth. I was Senior Class President of Scottsdale High in 1964 and my parents attended my graduation ceremony. One warm spring weekend several buddies, girlfriends and I drove up the back roads of Papago Peaks Park to Governor Hunt's (Arizona's first governor, in 1912) pyramid-shaped tomb on a small mountainside to drink beer and enjoy the spectacular night view. One of the guys knew that our necking spot overlooked the large back enclosure of the Phoenix Zoo, and while fooling around near the tall fence below in the dark, we managed to disturb one of the resident buffalo. Protecting his turf, the bull charged us and put a nice dent in the heavy chain-links, managing only to stun himself and give us a good scare. The bull buffalo never got loose and wasn't really hurt, but I made the fortunate slip of mentioning this little escapade to my father. The rest, as they say, is literary history.

Dad was always very, very interested in the tribal rituals of American youth! Glendon made me drive him back in daylight to the scene to scout the terrain. He imaginatively enhanced my true story by having the bull buffalo escape and get hit by a semi, whose angry driver forces the now-sobered student revelers to finish off the wounded beast, put him out of his misery, with tire irons and a baseball bat!

This rough tale of teenage brutality appeared in *Esquire* a year later (July 1965), prompting some critical letters to the editor. "Going to See George's" (the nickname we gave to the enraged buffalo) primal theme of awakening the predatory beast lurking in all men and women echoed William Golding's "man in a savage animal" theme in his tremendous international success, *Lord of the Flies*.

But his short story and the disturbed reader reaction to it got Glendon to thinking further, finally deciding he didn't agree with Golding's provocative premise. After letting his ideas simmer for a few more years and then reading about Arizona's annual buffalo "hunt" in the paper, back to the typewriter he went. In the one newspaper interview he gave to Teri Crawford of the *Prescott Courier* during the filming of the movie, Glendon said that after actually witnessing the disgusting slaughter of these noble animals:

He still had just an idea and not a story. He thought of what would happen if someone did let the beasts go, but he went through many possibilities before he hit on the boys. "It took three years for this idea to suddenly happen," he said. Swarthout compared the book to *Lord of the Flies* by saying that it is kind of a rebuttal. "This book has the idea that people are not bestial in nature. It is just the opposite of *Lord of the Flies*. The idea is, if you isolate boys with the right combination of circumstances, they will do great things. So much is now anti-hero. This is a 'yes' book."

And so the novel was published by Doubleday in 1970, and this uplifting, much more positive theme obviously struck a better cord with readers, as *Bless the Beasts* eventually became an international bestseller and has been continuously in print ever since.

Some students struggle to understand the author's use of "Little Boy Blue" for this novel's epigraph.

If you don't remember the opening lines of the famous children's nursery rhyme, it begins "Little Boy Blue, come blow your horn, the cow's in the meadow, the sheep's in the corn." And there *are* buffalo in this tale, cruelly penned up without food or water. But the "boy" (or future generations of American youth), who *should* look after these sheep (or buffalo) is "asleep," isn't aware of this annual state-sponsored buffalo harvest, this slaughter-in-the-making. For if teenagers in the good ol' USA were awakened to the fact of this brutal tragedy, they'd cry out in protest, just as the boys do at the searing conclusion of *Bless the Beasts*.

And American school kids did protest this so-called hunt when they read about it in this novel. For several years after *Bless the Beasts'* publication, the Arizona Game and Fish Department received so many outraged calls and letters that they took to responding with a form letter, typing in the school's name and classroom number and referring to Glendon's book and the new, "improved" regulations governing the still-active buffalo killing.

Readers always want to know if the six boys were based on kids Dad knew or were just made-up characters.

I described to my father some of the campers from wealthier families from the Midwest and East

I'd encountered during my four summers at Hidden Valley Ranch for Boys, and some of these boys were certainly his inspiration for the six Bedwetters. But with a master's degree and a Ph.D. in English literature, Glendon was also a thorough researcher, so he turned to one of his friends in academia for help. At the time, Dr. Willard Abraham was Chairman of the Special Education Department at Arizona State University, charged with training future teachers of emotionally handicapped and gifted children. Dr. Abraham lent or recommended a number of the best books then available dealing with the problems of disturbed kids. From this research Glendon gleaned the "bumping" technique of the boys huddling together and hugging for mutual support and encouragement, much like those utilized in the "encounter" sessions and transactional (T-group) therapies which were all the rage in psychotherapy back in the late sixties when *Bless the Beasts* was written. Bumping is also something buffaloes do for safety and mutual support.

In the interview he gave to the *Prescott Courier*, Glendon stated that "the boys in this story are a can of worms. To create these characters, I read several books on education and on unusual and gifted children. I combined the problems of the cases I read. Each one is a classic case of psychological problems."

There are a number of special schools, camps

and retreats across America which cater to and counsel emotionally disturbed kids either full-time or on an occasional basis, such as a summer camp. In every state there are also youth camps full of juvenile delinquents, both boys and girls, who are working off their lawful sentences. Many of these problem kids are emotionally disturbed and abused, the product of broken homes, poor schooling, involved with gangs and drugs, much like Teft in *Bless the Beasts,* who had already run afoul of the law in a string of car thefts. There also isn't a school district in this country which doesn't have special classes for slow learners, dropouts or especially obstreperous kids. My father corresponded with a number of teachers of problem teens across the country, who raved about *Bless the Beasts* and the effect this book had upon their "special" students. One of the key messages in *Bless the Beasts & Children* is that we must *all* try harder to be more tolerant and understanding of, even friendlier with, those among us who are somehow different, who display handicaps, mental or physical, of some kind. Just like we've all got to look out for and protect the innocent animals of this earth, of whose care we're left in charge.

The Bedwetters in this novel certainly weren't battered children in the physical sense; rather, they were spoiled and neglected by preoccupied parents who overindulged them with toys and treats instead of love, attention and discipline. These overly permissive attitudes were fairly common among parents who sired children in the late forties and fifties. Survivors of the Great Depression of the thirties and then deprivation during World War II, these newly prosperous couples showered their baby boomers with goodies and privileges they themselves didn't enjoy as kids, and their soon-spoiled brats took advantage of their parents' materialistic largesse, as kids generally do, smoking, drinking and driving their own cars at too early an age. Hard-working parents sometimes did "warehouse" their bratty teens at summer camp, and we certainly had our share of them at Hidden Valley Ranch, although I never witnessed or heard about any serious acts of vandalism or juvenile delinquency while there. Glendon certainly learned about and met a few of these yuppies-in-training, though, and his descriptions of these characters probably run similar to some of the pampered offspring of wealthy families you may have known.

In the end, though, this book's problem kids pull together to save another group of well-fed but largely forgotten animals who are about to be seriously abused—permanently.

A few readers have asked if Sid Shecker was a caricature of a famous comedian such as Sid Caesar or Shecky Greene.

Sid was actually based on the famous comedian Buddy Hackett. Buddy was appearing at one of the big hotels in Vegas for a few weeks one summer, and one fine day he drove his two sons down in his limo to Hidden Valley Ranch for a partial month's session out of the Nevada heat. Buddy stayed with us through lunch, after which he graciously (compulsively?) got up and entertained the campers with a fast fifteen minutes of a much sanitized version of his stand-up comedy routine. Buddy's boys got along fine, though, and by the end of their couple of weeks *had* learned to ride.

Many students are confused by Glendon's seemingly nonsensical use of the immortal opening verse of one of America's most famous folk songs, "Home on the Range." It *is* unusual and a bit of a stretch for a younger reader to grasp the symbolism, but when you think about it awhile, this nonsense verse makes perfect sense in this context: "Oh give me a home, where the buffalo roam, where the deer and the antelope play, where seldom is heard, a discouraging word, and the skies are not cloudy all day." Any writer telling a story about buffalo has got to work this tune in somehow. By the middle of chapter 19, all six boys are on the brink of nervous exhaustion. They have been up all night on a long and grueling horseback ride, truck ride and hike, with nothing to eat and very little to drink (almost like the poor buffalo they're attempting to free, penned up without food and water for three days.

It's one thing to *describe* characters as being exhausted and disoriented, but how do you *show* these boys to be in this confused mental state, to get inside these characters' heads? It's here that the author turned the song you know he's going to have to use somewhere in this story into recognizable gibberish symbolic of the delirium, the intense mental confusion, young men and beasts face in literally the last moments of their lives. "O twayne me a twim, where the ffubalo jym, where the rede and telopen zoom; where nibber is nat, a confamitous rat-tat-tat, and the dils are not icky all doom."

These buffalo aren't roaming free yet, on *this* bloody range and deer and the antelope don't play, the words we hear are *all* discouraging, and these skies definitely *are* cloudy.

Whole classfuls of kids became so worked up over the book's buffalo killing scenes that they wrote or called Glendon by conference phone, wanting to know who they could write or call to protest and to help halt Arizona's senseless slaughter of their two buffalo herds. Adults, too, joined the fray, not believing that the "festive" carnival of blood depicted in the novel could actually exist!

Sadly, my father described Arizona's annual three-day buffalo "hunt" in *Bless the Beasts* exactly as he'd witnessed it. Here's what that one *Courier* journalist reported.

As far as the idea of a buffalo hunt goes, Swarthout said he read an item in a newspaper about a buffalo hunt outside of Flagstaff. He was interested and decided to go as an observer. He said not many people know of these herds, but every year eighty of the animals are marked for eighty people whose lucky numbers are drawn for the hunt. With brilliant blue eyes flashing, he said, "I was sickened and astounded by the barbarous way these animals are killed. I can see it is necessary to thin the herd, as the range won't support large numbers, but I object to the way in which they are killed. What is in the book is a real and true depiction of this animal atrocity. The people who shoot these animals are called shooters, they are not hunters."

In his fine review of this novel for the *Saturday Review of Literature,* another famous author, Brian Garfield, supported Glendon's harsh criticism of this state-sponsored killing.

To summarize the plot would reveal surprises the reader should discover for himself. But perhaps it requires a note: One scene depicts a terrifying, mindless act of collective human savagery—a violent ceremonial murder of helpless animals. The scene is one about which I have heard strong disbelief expressed. But it is essential; you must accept it as an authentic observation of real human conduct, or dismiss the novel as a tissue of false analogies. Therefore I stress, from personal knowledge, that the episode describes a practice carried on in several Western states with ritual regularity, and that Swarthout pictures the slaughter accurately. What is appalling is that he didn't have to make any of it up.

When *Bless the Beasts* was published, the controversy really hit the fan. Besides a few knowledgeable reviewers like Garfield, the news media got onto the story and outraged readers began calling and writing Arizona's Game and Fish Department. *The New York Times* and *Sports Illustrated* weighed in with articles, and finally Governor Jack Williams called my dad to ask if this was true, if the hunt really was Arizona's dirty secret, the nearest bloody spectacle to a legalized bullfight any government body had ever sanctioned before in America!

Glendon was never a protester or a joiner of causes or organizations, but this so-called buffalo hunt so disgusted him that he gave impassioned testimony before a committee in the state legislature that was considering new legislation canceling the slaughter altogether. But it was not to be. The hunting and gun lobbies were just too powerful and politically well-connected. Killing a buffalo qualifies a hunter to be in the running for the Arizona Big Ten, which is a trophy given out every year by one of the ammunition makers to any sportsman who can bag all of the top-ten game animals in the state over the course of his hunting career. The Big Nine just wouldn't have quite the same sporting cachet. So a bureaucratic compromise was reached and the rules governing the hunt were altered. State game rangers now accompanied each lucky shooter out onto the range to deliver a quick-kill shot to any poor animal which a nervous marksman had only wounded. The great beasts were no longer penned but were still driven into shooting range by wranglers for the convenience of the customers.

In the fall of 1972, Stanley Kramer's film of the novel was released and protests against this atrocity increased. Kramer obviously didn't want to kill any buffalo for his movie, so documentary 16mm footage of one of these penned shoots taken by a hunter was purchased and blown up and "matched" with the locations used for the actual buffalo stampede in the movie's climax. Animal rights activists were now so incensed by the book and the film that for a couple of years they tried to disrupt this annual culling of the state-owned herds, promising to throw their bodies in front of the terrified animals. But too much income from the sale of game licenses was involved, not to mention financial contributions to the legislators by the ammunition and gun manufacturers. The passage of time and the modified hunting regulations slowly dampened the controversy, though, and the game wardens kept the shooting dates as little publicized as possible and kept protesters well away from the killing grounds.

And so the great state of Arizona's organized butchery continues every October. The fees change yearly depending on the surplus the herds' caretakers decide to get rid of. In 1993, sixty-three were culled. Shooters now have to hunt their animal by themselves on foot, after watching an instructional videotape so they can distinguish the size and gender of the animal they've paid for. The House Rock Ranch herd is hunted over the roughest terrain and pack horses are usually required to bring out these carcasses, for which the permit holders are responsible. Arrangements for butchering must also be made by the shooters. Law enforcement personnel are around to guide the shooters to the general hunting areas and to see that the proper animal is selected, but they no longer assist in finishing off wounded buffalos. Game and Fish personnel are pleased that it's now just like hunting any other big game animal, except, of course, for those sturdy fences containing the Raymond Ranch and House Rock Ranch herds.

It's a tragedy that this "hunting" farce is still allowed to continue, but I console myself with the thought that at least the spectacle has been removed from the slaughter. The buffalo now have the privilege of being blasted to bits in private just like every other American game animal. *Bless the Beasts,* however, has the distinction of being one of the few works of fiction I'm aware of that ever resulted in government regulations' being rewritten and caused such significant social outrage over an animal rights issue. In recognition of this fact, the members of the Ark Trust, an animal rights organization, voted Stanley Kramer's film of *Bless the Beasts & Children* a Genesis Award in its classic film category. The award was presented to the eighty-one-year-old director in 1994 in a ceremony televised on the Discovery Channel. Better late than never.

Significantly, George Meyer, one of the young producers who also won a Genesis Award that night—for an episode of *The Simpsons,* a popular animated TV series—stated in his acceptance speech that he'd seen the movie *Bless the Beasts & Children* as a kid and that it was his very first exposure to animal rights issues and certainly inspired him. This same story has undoubtedly been a big influence on the thinking and animal rights activism of millions of other young American readers and viewers over the past twenty-five years.

Numerous readers also wrote my father to ask if the religious parallels in *Bless the Beasts* were deliberate. Priests and pastors admired the book and asked him questions about his faith, his thoughts about the Creation. Whole classes from

Christian academies as well as secular schools got into debates over these religious inferences in the text.

Glendon was not a formally religious man, attending no church nor professing any specific faith. But he definitely espoused Christian principles, and he was certainly familiar with the Bible, which he felt was the greatest story ever told. The few religious references in the novel *were* deliberate, to help give this "exciting mission/pursuit story" a deeper resonance, a little more meaning.

John Cotton and Jesus Christ were both leaders who sacrificed themselves to free their people. Cotton organized his misfits, who, working together as a team, achieved something greater than themselves and their personal hangups: freeing the buffalo, America's endearing symbol of our frontier heritage and vanished past. "The *only* buffalo you'll ever see is on a nickel," so the saying went. Cotton also shares some liquor with his pals after they've first freed the buffaloes from their pens, and while this might be similar to Christ's sharing the sacrament of the wine with his disciples at the Last Supper, drinking whiskey is also something men often do with their buddies to buck up their courage or to celebrate a job well done.

Shecker's joke in the restaurant about their rock group, "Before Christ," is used merely to trick the mean cowboys, to keep them from realizing that the boys are actually from Box Canyon Boys Camp south of Flagstaff. Finally, calling a pickup truck a

"Judas" truck is a writer's way of personifying that vehicle and fixing in the reader's mind exactly how and for what purpose this particular truck is used.

So, no, I don't think John Cotton represented a Christ figure to Glendon or that he deliberately gave him the same initials as Jesus Christ. But again, this novel can be appreciated on many levels, and each reader is free to interpret it as he or she wishes. I just think some readers make too much of Christ comparison, but I sure wish I had the chance to question my father about these same issues.

Most readers will wonder whether Cotton's tragic death at the story's end is the result of an accident or suicide. In that one interview he gave, here's what Glendon said about it:

> I can't and won't justify the ending of this book. There could be many reasons why Cotton dies. It may have been the last best thing he could do for his friends by ridding them of his leadership. He sacrifices himself, just as he does the chamber pot.

Good stories make you think, don't they? So, readers of *Bless the Beasts & Children,* you'll just have to decide about Cotton's death for yourself.

Glendon Swarthout passed away on September 23, 1992, from progressive emphysema caused by his lifelong smoking. *Bless the Beasts & Children* was his masterpiece, and the effect this literary classic has had on its millions of avid readers is apparent from the hundreds of moving, impassioned letters his fans wrote to him over the quarter century his novel has been in print. Pocket Books' commemorative 25th anniversary edition of it is a fitting tribute to a creative genius, an amusing fellow and a truly nice guy.

Bless the beasts . . . and the children . . . and their creator . . . indeed.

Miles Hood Swarthout
Malibu, California

1

IN THAT PLACE THE WIND PREVAILED. THERE WAS ALways sound. The throat of the canyon was hoarse with wind. It heaved through pines and passed and was collected by the cliffs. There was a phenomenon of pines in such a place. When wind died in a box canyon and in its wake the air was still and taut, the trees were not. The passing trembled in them, and a sough of loss. They grieved. They seemed to mourn a memory of wind.

Cotton dreamed.

Six of them waited in early morning, held in a kind of enclosure behind thick posts and planks and bunched up not because they were afraid but because, unused to being penned, they were excited and, close together, they could communicate by odor. They snuffed one another. Through dilated nostrils they drew in the hot, animal odor of their excitement.

Then men came, horsemen. A gate was opened. Shouted at, they tried to stampede out together, but the gate was slammed after the lead three, Teft and Shecker and Lally 1, were through. The others waited. Soon the air was split by riflefire. It spooked the three remaining. They milled in circles, bending planks and sideswiping posts, unafraid yet more excited than ever, since it was a stimulus in the ear which they could not identify. In the after-silence they waited again.

The horsemen returned. The gate was opened and the last three, Cotton and Goodenow and Lally 2, were let out down a lane of wire fencing. It was good to be unpenned and free in the vivid morning. But when they paused to drink from a pond the horsemen harried them on, waving hats and shouting.

In an open field they made a stand. One hundred yards away a line of vehicles confronted them, and before the vehicles, a line of humans. Released earlier, Teft and Shecker and Lally 1 were nowhere to be seen. This puzzled them, as did the gunshot and Goodenow's going down, first to his knees, then folding his hindquarters, then heavily upon one side. He did not move. Cotton and Lally 2 snuffed the new strange odor emanating from the carcass.

At the next report Lally 2 leaped up and came down stifflegged, and at the other violences in the ear shook his head and toppled, his eyes glazed, his limbs doubling and extending convulsively and brilliant red blowing from his mouth and nose. Cotton snuffed the blood. This smell he knew.

One lunge sent him into top speed, running this way only to be turned by vehicles, running that way only to be hemmed in by horsemen. Snorting, he tried another, battering head down into a wire fence and recoiling upon his haunches. He bounded up, maddened by the obstacle of steel which must give way before him.

Raging, he stood. Omnipotent, glaring at the line of humans, he centered on the muzzle of a rifle and down the barrel and into the half-face of a woman seated on a tarpaulin sighting him. She fired. He recognized her. The microsecond's recognition shattered his heart even as her bullet broke his brain. It was the face of his mother.

Cotton woke with a cry.

His forehead, palms, and inner thighs seeped sweat. He disgusted himself. He was fifteen, the oldest, too old to have bad dreams.

He checked the time. It was five of eleven. He had been asleep less than half an hour. Hoisting himself on an elbow, out of habit he checked his personnel. Goodenow, Teft, Shecker, Lally 1—where was his brother? Then he remembered: Lally 2 had moved pillow and sleeping bag under his bed at lights out. In the seventh bed, Wheaties, their counselor, about whom no one gave a damn anyway, snored. All present, sir, and accounted for.

Cotton saluted himself and lay back listening to the sorrow of wind in pines outside the cabin and the pulsing of transistor radios inside. That was how they induced sleep, the other five, with their radios, the way puppies ceased to whimper and dozed off if you tucked a ticking clock in their boxes to represent another heartbeat. At lights out they slid into sleeping bags and tucked the tiny radios under their arms and turned them to the Prescott station for country & western or to the one in Phoenix for soul. At first the dark was full of twang and nasal lament for lost loves and defunct broncs or electronic incoherence about baby, baby, and the blues, but as they twisted in their sleep, as the radios worked down in the bags, the music fuzzed and faded until it was not music but a presence near their feet. Eddy Arnold kept them company, and Aretha Franklin. Through the night the radios pulsed, and they were not alone.

Mornings and evenings were their most difficult times. Mornings they were reluctant to leave the security of the sack. Goodenow groaned, Teft scratched, Shecker and the Lally brothers dawdled dressing as though the reality beyond the cabin lay in wait for them with fang and claw, crouched. Evenings they dreaded the coming of the dark, and with it emigration into dreams, the conscious sending away of conscious self into the unknown. They put it off as long as possible. Teft went to the latrine. Shecker talked. Goodenow read paperbacks and magazines by flashlight. Lally 1 threw things. They drank from canteens slung over bedposts. Shecker ate candybars. In the gloomy corners Goodenow poked for omens, using flashlight for fingers. On the bare cave walls of the cabin Lally 2 painted hieroglyphs in light, undecipherable messages to tomorrow. Now I lay me down to sleep, I pray the Lord my batteries keep. Evening was better for them now than it had been in the beginning. Cotton was proud of that. But it was still bad enough, and tonight they had slipped. This had been the worst of the summer.

They had returned in late afternoon from an overnight camp-out in the Petrified Forest. After washing up they went to supper in the chow cabin, forcing food down. No sooner were they outdoors again when in the midst of everybody, Goodenow vomited. He urped everything. *Goodenow wet the bed. He was driven from two cabins for it. Cabins were not assigned. Boys bunked where they wished at first, or where they could, by chance or hunch or necessity. In a few days, according to camp theory, everyone would find his group, his home far from home, and his achievement level as well, for the laws of temperament and competition inevitably separated the deviant from the normal, the losers from the winners. Let them alone and the thirty-six youngsters would divide themselves naturally into six teams, each with its own cabin and counselor. But even at fourteen Goodenow still wet the bed. He was also a sissy, and thumbs at everything except making Indian beadwork belts and headbands. He was also homesick and cried much and when, the second morning, he was driven from a second cabin, he put on swim trunks, went to the tank, a small artificial lake, waded in up to his chin, and stood sobbing an intention to drown himself. Neither counselors nor campers took him seriously. To demands that he duck and do it, he bawled that the water was too cold. Spectators rolled on the ground. When asked why he didn't suicide in his sleeping bag, which was wetter than the tank anyway, and certainly warmer, he splashed out of sight between canoes. He remained immersed until Cotton that afternoon talked him out of the tank with an invitation to join his cabin. There, he was assured, no one would laugh at him, and if anyone did, he, Cotton, would beat hell out of him.* How they passed the evening after Goodenow vomited, Cotton could not recall, except that it had been an evening unlike any of the summer. No one hung or horsed around. What they had witnessed during the day had traumatized them. They dared not discuss it. Like walking wounded they scuffed separately among the trees, hiding from one another in the twilight. For the first time they welcomed the onslaught of the dark.

At lights out the cabin became a ward. Lally 2 regressed under his bed. The others zipped themselves into sleeping bags as though into burrows, turning radios in and volume higher than ever before. There was no going to the latrine this night, no talking, no throwing things, no reading or eating or slurping from canteens or confession with flashlights. They fled into a sleep which was not repose. Now they could speak. Now all could upchuck what they had seen that day. They turned the night into an echo chamber. Goodenow thrashed. Teft ground his teeth. The Lally brothers chorused horror. Cotton dreamed of them being penned like beasts and murdered by their own parents. All of them cried out in a babble of id, ego, odor, blood, and the madness of men while Dionne Warwick ululated soul and Roy Acuff sang of sin and redemption. It was a catharsis by voice, and in vain.

Cotton listened again. Something was wrong. He counted off four radios, not five. Easing out of bed he peered under the bed beside his. Lally 2 was gone. Pushing feet into sneakers, he padded outside in his skivs and along the path to the latrine. Lights were on but the john was deserted, as was the shower room. More swiftly this time he jogged back to the cabin, and bending under the bed again found the half-burned foamrubber pillow Lally 2 had brought from home also missing. That cinched it. He stood for a moment shivering, knowing why but determined not to admit, even to himself, that he knew why.

He stepped across to Lally 1, put one hand firmly over his mouth, and with the other fist gave him a punch in the ribs. Lally 1 squirmed and grunted.

"Where's your brother?" Cotton whispered, removing his hand.

"Broken out."

"I know that. Where?"

Lally 1 told him, adding, "He said he was going and he did, so what."

Cotton was furious. Lally 1 was fourteen, his brother only twelve. "Don't you even care?" he hissed.

"No, I don't. It's no skin off mine."

"Well, I do and you better. How was he going—walk all the way there and back?"

"He said walk into town, then hitch rides."

"He's crazy. Okay, out of the sack. We're going after him, all of us."

"Not me."

"Yes, you, damn you, or I'll destroy you. Now move it. I'll wake the others."

Bed by bed, with hand over mouths and mutters to throw on clothes and move it, Lally 2 had taken off and they had to catch him, Cotton roused Teft and Shecker and Goodenow, who sprang sweating from the locked, tormented cells of sleep. Action offered escape. They seemed to know, as he did, why Lally 2 had gone, and where. And after what the day had done to them, the night could do no worse. By the time he pulled on pants and a T-shirt they were ready, following him out the door as stealthily as Indians and remembering, even, to leave their radios on to lull the counselor, Wheaties. Cotton was proud of them. They were finally showing him some smarts.

2

A BROOD OF CABINS NESTED IN THE PONDEROSA. AT an elevation of three thousand feet the great trees feathered them. Plain splitlog sides and shingle roofs outcropped it seemed from rock, thrust up here and there through a floor of granite shale and needle droppings.

Over this floor the five walked warily, circling the camp to reach the sand road which led up, then down the canyon throat into a piney woods a mile or more to the paved highway into town. Striking the road at the top of the rise they stopped. From here they could look down and back over the cabins and corral and tack barn and rifle range and ballfield and truck shed and tank. There were lights in the two latrines, but none in the cabins of the senior counselors or that of the Director. Beyond the camp the box canyon closed. A barricade of cliffs cut off the world. Higher than these, however, à range of Arizona mountains bulked, and then another higher, and another, a herd of huge black beasts plodding its patient way to a frontier not yet found, snorting clouds and bumping heaven with its humps and hooking stars upon its horns. It was the Mogollon Rim.

They gathered around Cotton.

"How long's he been gone?" Teft asked.

"Twenty minutes, half-hour. We have to grab him before he hits the highway. He gets a ride and zoom."

"I was sure one of us would go," said Goodenow, half to himself. "I didn't know who."

Shecker yawned. "He won't hurry, not him. He's doing his thing, he should care how long it takes."

"Okay, okay," Cotton said, "let's not dink around. We'll double-time to the highway. C'mon."

Off they went together at a trot, down the sand road winding through the woods, panting and pumping elbows in unison except for Lally 1, who lagged a little behind since it was his brat brother they were after. For five minutes they double-timed, in and out of stipplings of moonlight, the cadence of their footfalls muted by sand, till Cotton held them up and said to listen for the radio. He'd taken his pillow, so probably his radio, too. Listening, they heard the sounds of their breathing and the sorrow of the pines.

"No use." Lally 1 caught up with them. "He's nuts anyway."

Goodenow wheezed. He was the least strong. "We're too late. Our fault. We should've all gone."

"Knock it off," Cotton panted. "C'mon, move it."

He led them into a jog again, dogtags jingling round his neck, and away they double-timed, faster now. Goodenow's words whipped them. Guilt nipped at their heels. Around an S-curve they pounded, and were nearing the gate which marked the boundary of camp acreage when, simultaneously, they saw him, and Lally 2, tramping down the middle of the road, saw them. He froze, then darted into the woods.

"Get 'im!" Cotton gasped. "Fan out!"

Dodging trees they tore into the woods, chasing this way and that until, emerging from shadow into a clearing, they pulled up short. There was Lally 2, charred, smelly pillow under arm and radio pulsing in a jacket pocket, seated on a boulder looking at them and sucking his thumb. They would have pounced on him had Cotton not ordered them to hold it, he'd talk to the kid alone a minute. He walked on ahead.

"Hullo," Cotton said.

Lally 2 tightened hold on his pillow.

"Nice night, huh?" Cotton asked.

Lally 2 was twelve years old and not talking. *Of the sixteen rooms in his home in Kenilworth, Illinois, his favorite was the seventeenth, the Oom*

11

room. It wasn't really a room at all, but a sauna his father had built into the house and forgotten to use. His father and mother were young and beautiful people and had inherited "old money," third-generation wealth. Every year they separated once or twice, began divorce proceedings, then reconciled and jetted off to ski at Chamonix or somewhere or to yacht in the Virgin Islands or somewhere. It gave them a game to play. But while they were gone, the house, except for his older brother and the governess and maids and butler and chauffeur and cook, seemed lonely and empty. When he would have a bad dream and wake in the lonely, empty house, Billy Lally would take his foamrubber pillow and creep downstairs into the sauna and turn the temperature to 160 degrees and curl up on the wooden bench with his head on the pillow. Soon the Ooms, little people who lived under the flat rocks and made steam, would come out, hundreds and hundreds of them, and snuggle with him and help him to sleep safe and warm till a maid or the butler found him in the morning. Frequently he caught a cold from sleeping in the sauna, but to be warm and safe in the night was worth a cold. Billy Lally had never told anyone about his friends, the Ooms.

Cotton hunkered down opposite. What the boy had been exposed to that day had probably hit him harder than any of them, Cotton thought, since he was the youngest, and having withdrawn under his bed at lights out, Lally 2 was still under, even here in these woods. He would have to be gentled out.

"At least turn your radio down," Cotton said, "so you can hear me."

Lally 2 turned it down.

"Listen," Cotton said, "we do stuff together, not by ourselves any more." He tucked his dogtags under his T-shirt. "So let's go back now, what say?"

Lally 2 removed his thumb. "You make me go back and as soon's you're asleep I'll take off again. I mean it."

"What if I order you not to?"

"I don't care."

"You could have got hurt, Lally Two, really hurt."

"I don't care."

Cotton picked up a pebble, tossed it, caught it, dropped it. Looking over his shoulder, he raised an arm and waved the others over. They came and squatted. As perspiration dried on their bodies they shivered and hugged themselves to keep warm.

"Lally Two and I've been talking," he said. "He says if we make him go back he'll just take off again. I tried to tell him it's—"

"Don't you blame me!" interrupted Lally 2, unjustly accused. "We oughta all go! You been thinking about it, too, ever since we got back from there this afternoon. We oughta all go and you know it!"

They knew it. They had been obsessed from the moment Goodenow urped his supper, and later, walking alone, they mulled it, sealing themselves into envelopes of down and wool and nylon they could not hide from it, in sleep it was torn from their lips together with the gibberish of protest. It boiled in a boy's veins. It rocketed a boy's imagination into the outer space of impossibility. But more than a chance, more than a challenge, it was at the same time an obligation they were not sure they were experienced enough, that they had hair enough, to assume. Hunkered down in the piney woods, hugging themselves, they weighed the risks against what they had already accomplished in seven weeks: a midnight movie ridden to, a raid on the entire camp carried off, the race to the rim of the Grand Canyon.

"I gotta admit," said Shecker.

"If we could pull it off," Teft mused, "it would be the biggest."

"Yeah if," said Lally 1.

"We have to!" Goodenow burst out. "And I'm ready right now!"

Cotton stood up. "Hold your water. Let's not go off half-cocked. Use your heads—how'd we get there? Ride? A hundred miles one way?"

"Hitch," said Lally 2. "I was going to."

"Six of us? Who'd pick up six kids the middle of the night?"

"Take a truck," Teft said quietly.

"Hah. Who'd drive?"

"I would."

"You can drive?"

"Yup."

"Have you ever actually?"

14

"Actually. Give me wheels and I'm the Red Baron."

They were astonished. That anyone fourteen years old should for seven weeks have concealed an ability to drive a car was incredible.

"Oh," Cotton said. "Well. Okay, how long would it take, a hundred miles?"

"Two hours, about, each way."

"Four." Cotton figured out loud. "It must be eleven-thirty. Twelve, one, two, three—and say an hour to do it. Four-thirty we're back here. We have to be back in the sack again by daylight." He began to pace behind them.

"How about it?" Goodenow asked.

"We never miss," Shecker said.

"We have to go," said Lally 2.

"We're professionals," bragged his brother.

"Bullcrap," Cotton said.

Bending, he scooped up another pebble, and winding up, fired a bigleague fastball into the nearest tree. With a squawk and a whoosh, something flew out and over them, flapping wings. It scared them out of a year's growth. They flopped backwards or seized each other or leaped in panic, then recovered themselves and stood about like morons, stubbing the ground and grinning.

"That's what I mean," Cotton said scornfully. "A bird and we blow our minds. I don't know if we're ready for anything this big."

"We're not now, we never will be," Teft said.

"Okay, but compared to this, everything else

15

we've done was peanuts. We could get our ass in a sling on this. I'm serious."

He had a point. They were silent. Lally 2 turned off his radio. Worms of doubt worked in them. They could do miracles now, but Lally 1 could also recall the first pow-wow, and Shecker, the raid they had flubbed. Cotton would never forget himself on the pitching mound another time. Under the best of circumstances theirs was a tenuous, temporary association. Apply stress, demand a rational decision, flush a bird unexpectedly from a tree, and they came down with a fast case of the fidgets.

Box Canyon Boys Camp enrollment was drawn from the affluent metropolitan suburbs of the East and Middle West and restricted, with rare exceptions, to boys between thirteen and sixteen years of age. The fee for the eight-week session extending from late June to late August was sixteen hundred dollars, plus air fare. "Send Us a Boy—We'll Send You a Cowboy!" was the camp slogan. To this end each camper was assigned his own horse to ride and tend. The real means to this end, however, was competition. Boys they might come—immature, overprotected dudes with television for brains and smog for character—but men in the making they would go. Competition would hone them down and tall them up. Colicky yearlings they might have been, but competition and eight weeks and sixteen hundred dollars were guaranteed to deliver the goods their parents had bought and paid for: three dozen

*whipthin, deadeye, leathergut, spursharp, buttonlip
Westerners.*

By the end of the first week the enrollment had
indeed shaken itself down into six teams in the six
cabins. A natural selection of age and cruelty and
regionalism and kindred interest had begun the
process. Preliminary testing did the rest. Early trials
in riding, archery, riflery, crafts, swimming, and
field sports soon winnowed the wheat from the chaff,
the achievers from the ineffectual. It was to be
expected that any summer would single out a misfit
or two, an isolate here, an emotionally disturbed
there, but Cotton's group was unique. They moved in
with him because no one else would have them. They
were known variously as the Weirds, the Screwups,
the Locos. They were the bottom of the barrel.

When they came to bat in their first baseball
game, for example, they failed to score. They
couldn't hit a bull in the behind with a bushel basket.
When they took the field, Cotton pitched, Shecker
caught. Lally 1 played first base, Goodenow third,
Teft went to left, and Lally 2 to right field. It was the
funniest athletic event the camp had ever seen.
Behind the plate, Shecker ducked pitches rather than
catching them, claiming Cotton threw too hard and
hurt his hands. Easy grounders dribbled through
Lally 1 and Goodenow as though through a sieve.
Teft misjudged a fly ball to deep left, disappeared
into the pines after it, and never returned. Lally 2
dropped a pop fly, sat down on the ground, and

17

sucked his thumb. When the score was 21–0 and the stands hooted, Cotton charged into them, attacked two boys twice his size, got a loose tooth and a bloody nose for his efforts, and the game was over.

"This is one show I'm not ramrodding," Cotton told them. "We're gonna vote. Think it over—today's Tuesday, the last week, and we go home Saturday, we go home winners. So if we try this, nothing or nobody stops us. So you be sure."

He gave them a minute, then cleared his throat. "Okay, we vote. Everybody has to be for it. Everybody or we don't go. Okay, all in favor raise your right hand."

It was unanimous.

"What about you?" piped Lally 2.

"Yeah," the others said, "what about it?"

Cotton came among them, holding back, and they bunched up around him in the dark woods, shivering and uncertain until, that close, they could almost smell his pride in them, his excitement and desire. Then he let them have it, his voice low but so charged with passion that it prickled the hair on their heads.

"You damn betcha. Let's go, men."

18

3

THEY CHAMPED AT THE BIT. THEY WOULD HAVE double-timed again but Cotton marched them back along the sand road, telling them to save their hots, they would need them before this night was over, with a finger testing his loose tooth and thinking.

On the rise overlooking camp he gathered them. "This is like a guerrilla operation," he said, "or a patrol or something. We've gotta plan it and time it and everybody do his part. First, we get dressed— and dress warm, because it's three thousand feet higher up there, it'll be cold as a witch's tit. Bring your flashlights and anything else you want, I guess, if we're taking a truck. Circle, don't let anybody see us. I'll give you guys five minutes to be in the truck shed ready to go. Any questions? Okay, spread out and move out."

Lally 1 tried to sneak a letter home. It would not have reached his parents in any case, since they had just reconciled and shipped their sons to camp and jetted off for a camera safari in Kenya. Cotton caught him and tore up the letter. Stephen Lally, Jr., had a temper tantrum. Screaming at the top of his lungs he rose from his bed on hands and knees and rocked, butting his head against the wall. The others went to supper without him. When they returned, he had killed all the pets. Goodenow's lizards and beetles and spiders and snake, which he kept in cardboard boxes under his bed, Stephen Lally, Jr., had let out and stomped on the floor. His brother Billy's pets were a hoptoad and a baby rabbit, the latter crippled because one of its hind legs had been partially bitten off, probably by a coyote. The hoptoad he squashed, the baby jackrabbit he cornered and, pretending it was his baby brother, battered to death with a branding iron.

One by one they deployed through the trees, roundabout the chow cabin to their own. Wheaties sawed wood as raucously as ever. Cotton was first outside again, and chose a route by the cabin of the Comanches, taking cover between pine boughs to evade a boy sleepwalking to the latrine, then behind the crafts cabin to the truck shed where he waited, tugging impatiently at the chin strap of the army helmet liner he had bought in a surplus store in Cleveland. Eventually, one after another the rest lurked into the moonlight. They were dressed in what was almost the camp uniform: blue jackets with BC in white letters on the backs, wool shirts under, Levi's slim in the leg and tight in the crotch with concho belt buckles, sweat sox, and cowboy boots. But he could tell them apart by their headgear. It was the fashion that summer to affect freak headgear. Goodenow wore a Hopi headband he had beaded himself; Shecker a golf cap, bassackward, given to his father by Arnold Palmer after a round at Palm Springs; the Lally brothers expensive, identical ten-gallons, the wide brims of which, broken by rain and neglect, sagged over their ears; while Teft was made even taller by a billed Afrika Korps cap he had dug up in Greenwich Village.

As soon as Teft joined them, Shecker went as usual into his James Cagney impersonation, hissing, "Ah, you dirty Kraut! You dirty, dirty Kraut!"

Cotton shushed him, then noticed Lally 2 had his pillow, which was unnecessary enough, but also that Goodenow had lugged along the buffalo head, which was stupid. "Do you have to bring that?"

Goodenow pouted. "You said anything we want. And we've only got three more days to keep it."

Cotton shrugged. He asked Teft which pickup to take, the Dodge or one of the two Chevys. Teft whispered it made no difference to him, they all had keys.

"I didn't know they leave the keys in."

"I did. I keep an eye on keys. Anyway, who'd take a truck?"

They settled on the Dodge, stowed pillow and buffalo head and flashlights in the bed, and with

Teft in the cab, experimenting clutch and gearshift into neutral, they pushed the truck out of the shed. It was agreed they must push it through the pines and up and along the sand road far enough to start the engine without waking anyone.

It was easy going past the chow cabin and the counselors' cabins and the Director's, and the five of them managed enough momentum to run the Dodge halfway up the rise, but no further. Teft jumped out to help. Grunting, they pushed heads down, twelve hands against the tailgate, boots delving into sand, but could not toil the truck another inch. Shecker advised starting the engine and barreling away and being long gone before anyone could react. Cotton muttered not to be a damn fool, they'd be followed for sure or the police called or something. They strained against the pickup for minutes it seemed, and as they tuckered out, as despair sapped them more quickly, even, than exertion, one by one they dropped out, winded, till only Cotton's intransigence held the vehicle in place.

They waited, saying nothing, watching the silent struggle between his will and a ton of iron. He knew they had given up, sensibly, but he would not. His body arched, quivering, bent like a bow between irresistible truck and immovable earth. His helmet liner fell off. They feared Cotton a little at times like these. He was seized. He had fine frenzies. His motor control stuck, he scattershot his aggression at gods too indifferent to defeat, and his refusal to face the hard facts of night and day and weak and strong and life and death and gravity bordered on the psychotic. He was redheaded.

Competition continued throughout the second week under a point scoring system. Scores of the six teams in riding, archery, riflery, crafts, swimming, and field sports were posted daily on a bulletin board at the chow cabin and totaled Saturday afternoon. That night the first powwow was held in the pines near the rifle range. Around a pungent mesquite fire the boys and counselors gathered, and the Camp Director explained the naming of tribes and the award of trophies. Scores would be kept for the remaining six weeks of the session. At the powwow each Saturday night the teams, to be known henceforth as tribes, would be christened and awarded trophies on the basis of points scored during that week. The highest-scoring tribe would be the Apaches, and with that name and rank would come certain perquisites of achievement—an evening trip into town to see a movie, for instance, and watermelon for dessert. After the Apaches, in descending point order, would follow the Sioux, the Comanches, the Cheyenne, and the Navajo. The name of the last, or sixth-place tribe, he would reveal later.

He wished to emphasize, the Director said, that the rankings, and therefore the tribal names and trophies, were up for weekly grabs. With enough desire and elbow grease, any tribe might displace any other, and conversely, should it slack off, might fall off a notch or two in the standings. Incentive was thus inherent in the system, as it was in the American way of life. If you wanted to be Apaches badly enough, you could. If you wanted to avoid the ignominy of being low boys on the totem pole, you might. It was up to you. And now, he said, if the leader of the top team, now the Apaches, would step forward, he would present the trophy.

One of the older, larger boys entered the firelight. From behind a tree the Director brought the head of a huge buffalo bull, with horns and beard, its glass eyes redballed and fierce, its nostrils distended, and handed it over.

The Sioux received the head of a mountain lion; the Comanches, the head of a black bear.

To the Cheyenne and Navajo were given, respectively, the heads of a bobcat and a pronghorn antelope.

The Director then asked for a representative of the team in last place. Cotton stepped forward and was presented with a large white chamber pot. By camp custom, the Director announced, the team in last place on points was not honored with an Indian name. Instead, to activate its progress up the ladder of achievement, it was traditionally called the Bedwetters.

Cotton's body unstrung. He raised his head. Teft reached into the cab and set the truck in gear just as Cotton let go of the tailgate, picked up his helmet liner, and put it on.

"Cotton?"

"Yo."

"What say we saddle up and ride into town," Teft suggested easily, carefully.

"Then what?"

"I'll get us wheels."

"How?"

"Bag 'em."

"Steal a car?"

"Rent it. I mean, use one for a few hours and bring it back and leave some coin in it. For gas and mileage." All of them had ample pocket money.

"You should be locked up."

But the idea let air into the tension. They crowded in on Cotton, clamoring in whispers, being silly.

"How 'bout we bag two and race?"

"You said nothing stops us!"

"Teft—what a crook!"

"Let Teft put you in the driver's seat, heh-heh," Shecker cracked.

"Pipe down," Cotton hissed. "Teft, can you actually steal a car?"

"Actually, just call me Clyde."

They giggled.

"Pipe down." Cotton rubbed imaginary stubble on his chin. "Bag a car, bring it back. Maybe that's the only way, though. Okay, let's get this damn pile of junk back in the shed."

It was short work to let the truck roll down the rise, and after that, Teft steering, to push it into its slot. Lally 2 unloaded his pillow, Goodenow the buffalo head, and in a group they headed for the tack barn to saddle up. The camp was lifeless except for the lights in the latrines. Halfway, however, rounding one of the great pines, over the wind sound they heard a screen door squeak open and bang shut. They did statues. Cateyed, they made out the silhouette of a man standing on the stoop of a cabin, and a firefly. It was the Camp Director, smoking a cigarette. They had not known he smoked. He seemed to stare directly at them. They could not move a muscle until the firefly described an arc and the door squeaked open and banged shut again. They went on weak in the knees.

4

I N THE BLACK OF THE TACK BARN THEY FUMBLED among the baled hay and buckets and horse apparatus for bridles and blankets and saddles, then toted them into the corral. The animals knew them and behaved themselves.

Cotton cinched up, standing near enough to Teft to whisper. "You sweating this?"

"Are you?"

"Damn right. If we hadn't happened to see that sign today and turned off. And then Lally Two breaking out. And the truck. I don't want to blow everything this close to going home. We voted, sure, but they don't know what they're taking on. We could wreck the whole summer."

"It's wrecked anyway. Unless we swing this."

27

Cotton flipped stirrups down. "You were grinding hell out of your teeth tonight."

"I heard you holler yourself. Have a bad dream?"

Cotton skipped that. "I guess we have to go."

"Yup."

They were through the corral gate when Teft held them up with a handwave, signaling to wait, gave Lally 1 his reins, and leaned away on long spider legs. He was gone several minutes, returning, to their surprise, with one of the .22 caliber bolt-action target rifles from the range. Then in single file they led the drowsy horses through the pines around the perimeter of the camp, cautiously over shale and needle droppings to join the sand road, and down the road a hundred yards before Cotton stopped them.

"Teft, why'd you bring that gun?" he demanded.

The others chortled. "Let's rob banks, Bonnie, baby!"

"Kill! Kill!"

"You'll never take me alive, copper!"

"You get ammo?"

Teft rattled a box of cartridges.

"I thought they keep that rack locked now," Cotton said.

"They do."

Cotton shook his head and checked his wrist. "Eleven forty-eight. We're already behind schedule. Okay, mount up and move it."

They climbed aboard, reached into jacket pockets, snapped transistors on, and clucked the string into a trot. They were no cowboys. None of them had been born to the penthouse of a horse. Seven weeks of practice, though, had taught them how to cover the ground even if ungracefully, even if they snubbed the reins too short and rubbed horsehide raw with their knees and the slap-slap of their hind ends on saddles sounded like applause. Motion got their blood moving. The sand road kept their secret. To ride out against the rules, to ride out on a night of moon and mystery with high purpose for a theme and hooves for a beat and a counterpoint of creaking leather and Johnny Cash mooing "Don't Take Your Guns to Town"—to a boy this was wine and watermelon, first kisses and fireworks, liniment and delight.

The biggest entrance in the history of Box Canyon Boys Camp was that made by Sammy Shecker. He came down from Las Vegas in a limousine with his father, Sid Shecker, the famous comic, who was doing a month in Vegas and a month at Tahoe and decided a summer in the Arizona mountains would be healthier for his son than one cooped up in hotel air conditioning. As the chauffeur attended to the boy's things, Sid and Sammy inspected the camp facilities, Sid puffing a panatela and Sammy biting his fingernails. Sid even stayed for lunch, making jokes about the availability of kosher food in the Wild West, and after lunch did a benefit standup half-hour while Sammy, who was already fat, had

29

*seconds and thirds of everything on the menu. All the
campers had seen Sid Shecker on television, and
although his material was largely lifted from that of
other Jewish funnymen, his Arab-motherhood-Nazi-
bagel-Brooklyn routines broke them up. Leaving
them laughing, Sid went into the kitchen, tipped the
cooks $20 each so Sammy shouldn't starve, took a
counselor aside and tipped him $50 so Sammy
should always have a friend, and offered the Director
$100 so Sammy should have the best horse in the
corral. This the Director refused, but there were no
hard feelings and after spraying several ethnic one-
liners for a boffo finish, the comedian roared off in
his leased limousine and a chutzpah of dust.*

Around the S-curve, where they had earlier
caught up with the runaway, they posted, and came
to the wooden, roadwide camp gate. The rest
reined in as Cotton, bending, unlatched the gate
and rode it open. But they did not proceed. They
treated themselves to a moment. It was as though
they felt a redhot revelation coming on.

Under his army helmet Cotton reviewed his
troops. Under the headband and golf cap and
Afrika Korps cap and tramp ten-gallons they
gauged him, then glanced at the burnt pillow under
the arm of Lally 2, at the head of the bull buffalo
between Goodenow's thighs, at the rifle barrel
pointed over Teft's pommel, and then, longest, at
each other. They were impressed. One was fifteen
years old, four were fourteen, one was twelve. But

they were tremendously impressed, by themselves and by what they were about to attempt.

They were mad for western movies. They doted on tales told with trumpets and ending in a pot of gold, a bucket of blood, or a chorus of the national anthem. The finest movie they had lately seen, the only one that summer in fact, was *The Professionals*. It had been a buster, a dollar-dreadful, a saga of some men expert with weapons, a handful of colorful, heroic characters who rode into Mexico on a mission of mercy—to rescue a voluptuous babe from the clutches of bandits who had abducted her for foul, they were sure, purposes. It was a fundamental film, they knew it in their souls, a yarn innocent and scabrous, brutal and principled, true and a liar, as old as the hills and as new as the next generation. You did not watch it. You sucked on it. For this is the marrowbone of every American adventure story: some men with guns, going somewhere, to do something dangerous. Whether it be to scout a continent in a covered wagon, to weld the Union in a screaming Wilderness, to save the world for democracy, to vault seas and rip up jungles by the roots and sow our seed and flag and spirit, this has ever been the essence of our melodrama: some men with guns, going somewhere, to do something dangerous.

And so they were.

They looked at each other. Cotton grinned, ear to ear. Teft, Shecker, Goodenow, and the Lally brothers grinned at him. He nodded and gigged his horse about before them. They battened down their hats. Suddenly, as one man, they lashed with reins and banged the outraged animals in the bellies. Away the Bedwetters went, charging through the gate and over the silver screen and into history like cavalry. "Eee-yah! Eee-yah!" they yelled. "Eee-yah!"

5

THEY BOOTED AT FULL GALLOP UNTIL THE NAGS, unaccustomed to such shenanigans, were near collapse. Lally 2 had also dropped his pillow and would not go on without it. They waited for him near the paved highway into town, thanking their lucky stars they still had arms and legs, then swung right and let the animals weave at a drunkard walk along the gravel shoulder of the highway, blowing hard and slobbering.

One morning last autumn Goodenow was gripped by a phobic reaction to school. He could not enter his classroom. His breathing was labored, his state one of extreme fright. Interviewed by the principal, he disclosed fear for the safety of his mother, alone at home without him. He was passed on to the school psychologist, who quickly diagnosed the oedipal relationship. When he was four, Gerald's father died, and for eight years he slept with his mother. When he was twelve, his mother married an executive of a machine tool company in Cleveland, an engineer who had adult children of his own. The psychologist recommended therapy for Gerald and both parents. A man too old and preoccupied to be father to a young boy, the stepfather refused, but seen in private the mother revealed major ambivalence, a fragmentation between hostility and love, between the natural needs of a son and a new mate. Gerald's phobia intensified, as did his dependence on his mother. Placed in a special day school for emotionally disturbed children in Shaker Heights, where he lived, he underwent therapy. At the first sign of improvement, his stepfather enrolled him again in his regular school. The problem reappeared. He was unable to remain in the classroom. When his stepfather discovered that he wet the bed, he was severely punished.

They wrangled about what kind of car to bag. Shecker and Lally 1 were of the opinion that while you were at it, you might as well bag a Caddie or Imperial or Lincoln at least, but Cotton said no, six boys in a big car would stick out like sore thumbs. What they needed was a car nobody would notice, a nothing car.

"I was talking with the Director, one day after we took off for the movie," he said. "He told me we're juvenile delinquents the second we leave camp without permission. We can be picked up and tossed in the old hoosegow."

They wanted to know how come.

"Because by the law, a JD's anybody under sixteen who breaks the law or's a fugitive from his parents. That's the catch. He's our parents for the summer, acting as. If we break out, we're fugitives from our folks. He told me the camp's got it fixed that way with the fuzz. So bloodhounds and stuff."

A car passed them, and in the glare of its headlights they hunched down into jackets and up into headgear.

"Damn," Cotton swore. "We gotta get wheels fast."

He kicked his mount into a trot and the others followed him along the two-lane blacktop coiling in snake curves toward town. The first possibility they came to was a cocktail bar before which three cars were parked. They pulled up to consider.

"Take your pick," Teft said spaciously.

Cotton shook his head. "Unh-unh. That bar'll close in an hour. We grab one of those and the guy coming out'll see it's gone and call the cops and we'll have them after us. By radio."

They went on. Another car approached, this time from the front, and catching them fullbeam in its lights, braked sharply, swerving for a look at the nightmare parade beside the road. When it moved on, Cotton cursed again and ordered everybody off and lead horses, they had to ditch these animals. Trailing after him they left the highway, stumbling into a patch of greasewood and stunted trees. Here they tied up and bade farewell to their noble steeds, which were asleep on their feet anyway, then stumbled out again. Soon they entered civilization, the ragged commercial edges of Prescott, clomping past billboards and antique shoppes and rock shops and gas stations and curio emporiums and junkyards and coming eventually to a motel and its adjunct stable of automobiles.

"This is it," Teft said, handing over the rifle. "Those cars'll be there till morning."

Cotton agreed. "Okay, we split up. You bag one and we'll keep a lookout over there, by that Richfield station. And everybody turn off those damn radios."

They moved across the street and squatted behind a rack of retread tires while Teft sauntered among the travelers' cars, taking his time, appraising the various models with a dealer's cynicism. But as he stopped by a sedan, having a glance at the rubber, a car with a California license putzed out of nowhere and swung into the motel entrance and a man got out and stretched and rang the bell and lights blared on in the office and the man went inside to register, during which sequence Teft disappeared, to stroll a minute later across the street as though out for some fresh air. They huddled behind the retreads.

"Want to wait?" he asked Cotton.

"No. He'll have to park and unload and we don't have the time. Damn the lousy luck."

"We'll find something down the street."

"We better."

They did. Traipsing along, in less than a block they walked into a banquet of transportation—a used car lot. This time they accompanied Teft, only to find that the cars were locked and his skills, he confessed, did not include breaking and entering. Up and down the rows they scattered, trying doors, searching for a lowered window, and had worked their way to the rear of the lot when, without warning, the one police car in Prescott poked its hood into the drive and swiveled its spotlight from one side of the lot to the other. They ducked, they dove under cars, they embraced rear bumpers, and when, satisfied, the cop car pulled away, they dashed out of the lot like amateurs, running another block and ganging up under a streetlight. Frightened, angry with themselves because they were, they jumped first on Teft.

"Some crook!"

"The big-time car bagger!"

"You couldn't steal candy from a baby!"

"Whattaya need? The keys?"

Anxieties like mosquitoes beset them. And when Teft would not defend himself, they began to come apart at the seams as a team, to divide themselves into individuals, each with his own bulging jacket of concern and idiosyncrasy. It was this disintegrative behavior pattern, this overreaction to mistake or hindrance or minor misfortune, this rollercoaster drop from assurance to despair about which Cotton worried most. Over the short run, he was certain, the Bedwetters could now cope, but they were not yet prepared, temperamentally, for the long, hard pull. It was his flaw, too.

"We're great, yeah, we're really great," he sneered despite himself.

"I'm hungry," Shecker said.

Goodenow was near tears. He put down the buffalo head. "I can't carry this any more, my arm's tired. It's everybody's, and everybody should take turns."

"How we gonna do what we're supposed to if we can't even get there?" Lally 1 demanded.

"I'm hitching a ride," announced Lally 2, clutching his pillow. "Somebody'll give me one, because I'm just a little boy."

"Thumbtime," his brother taunted.

"No, bump time," Cotton said. "C'mon."

It was the magic word. Gladly they followed him out of the light and onto the sidewalk and under the overhang of a supermarket.

There they formed a circle, joined hands, and tightened themselves into a huddle, excluding the world.

They closed eyes.

They clasped arms about waists and shoulders and hugged.

Heads together, eyes closed, they bumped cheeks and noses gently, touching faces with their fingers.

Like blind boys they found each other, and confirmed each other, and through the FM of the flesh they sent to one another impulses of courage and affection.

Bumping was what they often did in an emergency.

"Hey," Teft said, breaking it up. He faced the street. Opposite them was the low, dark cube of a body shop, and parked beside it, in shadow, a white Chevy pickup perhaps ten years old, a muddy, fenderbent puddlejumper very similar to those at camp. "Will that do?" he asked Cotton.

"Hell yes. Anything that'll get us there." He pounded a fist into a palm, challenging. "Let's see you do it, though. We just wanna see you."

"Roger." Teft passed him the .22. "You gents wait down the street. I'll be along in a trice."

But they had to watch a car being bagged. Besides, they wanted to believe in Teft, to be astonished by him again, and rather than waiting down the block they scooted behind a Chevron billboard nearby, their heads sprouting from the frame like cabbages.

Old Teft moseyed across the silent street as though he wore a Colt and a tin star. Idling around the pickup, he made certain it was unlocked and the keys gone. He kicked a couple of tires. Approving, he stepped efficiently to the front end and raised the hood.

From a jacket pocket he extracted a jumper wire about eighteen inches long, with alligator clips at each end. Head and shoulders under the hood, he attached one clip to the positive terminal on the battery, the other to the battery connection on the coil. Lowering the hood, he opened the cab door and slid in.

On pickups this old, the starter button was on the dash, to the left of the steering column. His fingers reached it, pressed.

Teft often astonished them. He was tall, thin, and fourteen, though tall enough to be sixteen, a tilted boy who walked around with a tilted smile and said and did little and then, suddenly, said and did a great deal. There was something culpable about Teft. You suspected him first. He lived a tilted life. It was Teft who freed them from their junior counselor, the overgrown cornball of nineteen whom they called Wheaties because he had been a football hero in some nothing town in Arizona and rode well and was a sureshot with a rifle and attempted to peptalk them into shape—his shape—and in general made a fatuous, all-round horse's ass of himself. He hated them and they hated him, but Teft hated him more. To Teft, authority was tyranny, and one night, while Wheaties was in town on his night off, Teft put a lizard in his sleeping bag. When he returned, around one in the morning, and stuffed himself into bed, Wheaties hit the ceiling. He roared terror, then rage. He turned on the lights. He confiscated their radios. The other counselors said they were emotionally disturbed. He said emotionally bullcrap. What they really were was dings. A ding, he said, was something or somebody which didn't fit anything or anywhere. It used up space but it was useless.

Nobody wanted it or knew what to do with it. Therefore it had no excuse for being or living. And the six of them were the pee-poorest assortment of snotnose, big-mouth, crybaby dings ever enrolled in this camp and the only reason he had their cabin was because no other counselor would take it but he had a crawful now and from now on they'd toe his line or he'd disturb their goddam emotions so much the men in white coats would come take them away to the funny farm, where they belonged.

Hell he would, Teft said. Curling from his sack he dragged the footlocker from under Wheaties' bed and threw it open. Before Wheaties could stop him, he exposed the contents. Besides clothing there was a pint of whiskey, two six-packs of beer, a carton of cigarettes, and a stack of sex magazines. Wheaties yelled his locker was locked and personal. Teft replied he was expert with locks.

"So this is it, Wheaties," he said. "First, let's have those radios back. After that, you can play like our counselor but you won't be. Unless you want me to inform the Director what a fako you really are, what a bad influence, and how having you around might destroy our morals. And also what's in this locker." Teft smiled that tilted smile. "So from now on, baby, kiss off. You can live here, we'll let you because we're generous, but this is our cabin and we'll run it our way. And if you don't like it, you can shove it up your anal orifice."

The engine turned over, started, hiccoughed, stopped, started again, and settled down. Listening to it almost medically, Teft hooked a bootheel over the clutch, shifted by guess and gosh and bucked away from the body shop. He preferred automatic transmissions.

Gunning a full block before he spotted them tearing out from behind the billboard, chasing him, he braked, ground the gears into reverse, backed up to meet them in the middle of the street, braked again, and as they reached him, stuck an arm upright out the window, grinning. *"Achtung!"*

They were rapturous. All five tried to climb in beside him.

"Hey, Teft, how'dja do it?"

"Ladies first!"

"The Phantom strikes again!"

"Let's go to Disneyland instead!"

"Shut up, dammit!" Cotton cried. "Where d'you think you are? Okay, Lally Two and me in front, the rest in back—we'll change off later. C'mon, hurry up and shut up!"

They scrambled in, Lally 2 in the cab with him, Shecker and Goodenow and Lally 1 and the buffalo head in the bed. "Now listen, hear this," Cotton told those in back. "Lie down. Flat. We've bagged a car and we're armed—we're in real trouble if anybody stops us. You saw that prowl car. So stay down and no talking till we're out of town. Don't even breathe."

While they flattened out he ordered Lally 2 off the seat and on the floor, he wanted only a driver showing, and when Lally 2 was down, he laid the rifle on the seat and scrouged beside him, bowing head under the dashboard and closing the door. "Teft," he said, "you really know how to drive this thing?"

"I'm learning."

"Well. Take it slow—but not too slow. The thing is to get through town without anybody giving us a second look. A pickup with one guy driving and keeping his nose clean. Oh, and Teft, how about turning on the lights?"

"Lights? Geez, I forgot." Teft found the control and clicked the dimmer button on the floorboard.

"You guys aren't so sharp," sniffed Lally 2 under the dash, hatbrim over his nose. "Neither of you."

"How come?"

"I can't even see, but I bet Teft's still got that German cap on."

Teft grimaced and took it off and raced the engine. "Ready, skipper?"

"Fire one," Cotton said.

Teft geared the Chevy away smoothly this time, asking Cotton whether to stick to side streets or bluff it out on a main drag. Straightaway, Cotton thought, to save time and because it might look more suspicious if they monkeyed around on back streets. This one was Montezuma. They followed it downtown, to the stretch known in the good old days as Whiskey Row, a block of swing-door bazaars in which hard liquor was dispensed, two drinks for two bits, beer for a nickel, free lunch for indigestion, piano music for an earache, a poker hand for a silver dollar, and a close shave by .44 slugs for nothing: the Kentucky, the Wellington, the Del Monte, Cobweb Hall, and the Palace. It went up in smoke in 1900. Now, when greenhorn campers came into Prescott for an hour's spree every two weeks, they barged into a drugstore, spraddled up on soda stools, and exchanged decadent eastern paper for malts and nut sundaes and milkshakes and double banana splits.

"Holy cow," Teft said.

"What?"

"The law. That prowl car again."

"Sit tall," Cotton said.

On the floor then tensed until Teft puffed out his cheeks and whistled relief.

The pickup paused for a stoplight at the intersection of Montezuma and Gurley. On its right was the town plaza, a grassy square surmounted by the grass mass and clock tower of the Yavapai County Courthouse. A horse and rider reared upon a granite boulder. It was the equestrian monument to Bucky O'Neill, gay blade and sheriff and faro player and mayor of Prescott and captain of Troop A, First U.S. Volunteer Cavalry, Rough Riders, immortalized by Spanish lead at San Juan Hill and knighted now in bronze. The plaza was beautiful. Hawthorne trees cast pleasant shade in summer, and to the benches under the trees old codgers came daily from the veterans' hospital and the pioneers' home. Domiciliary patients, they were called, not ill or maimed or dotty enough to be confined but too infirm to tap with canes through a society which honored them with pensions and forgot to attend their funerals. In Hawthorne shade and to the tolling of the courthouse bell they mustered every day, these fragile warriors, sitting on the benches hour by garrulous hour, cussing and discussing an agenda of dentures and generals, surgery and ingrate daughters, taxes and the Old Testament, politics and final resting places— jogging memory with oaths and basing argument upon a bibliography of broken wind. They spat. They whittled. Waving tobacco cans, they cackled at pretty girls. Boys they dismissed with a fine misanthropy. Righteous and grand, they were also pathetic. They were dusty bugles, hungry for new lips. They were notes from the past adrift in cracked bottles, praying fair skies and kindly shores.

"Teft?" When they had turned onto Gurley and were headed up the hill and out of town, Cotton spoke.

"Yo."

"Bagging this crate. Damn well done."

"Thanks."

They began to roll. The Chevy ran hot and misfired on a cylinder or two and the front wheels wobbled out of alignment and the safety chains on the tailgate rattled unmercifully, but it would do. Leaving the last of the neon they connected with the state highway, curving north past the veterans' hospital on the site of what was once Fort Whipple, then on into bubbles of rock rising like yeast. When they took the right fork and were delivered, all at once, into wide open range, it was bye-bye cops, sleep tight Box Canyon Boys Camp, *adios* Prescott, and they were safe. The three flat in the bed came to life and pounded exuberantly on the cab window and Cotton and Lally 2 untangled onto the seat and pounded back and the Bedwetters cheered.

6

It was 12:35 by Cotton's wrist. Teft clapped on his Afrika Korps cap and said they could be there in two hours. "Sooner if I gun it."

"Lessee. Two-thirty there, half-hour for the job, three o'clock—home at five A.M. That's tight as hell," Cotton said. "Gun it."

They really rolled. Over a two-lane road as white and true as the part in a dude's hair they traversed range open as far as the eye could see, twenty treeless, houseless, humanless miles of it. But there was much moonlight. Out in the distances the fans of windmills twinkled, turning, and about the base of each, about the drink tank, was a speckle of dark dots, a gather of cattle grazing in moonlight and meditating upon good grass, block salt, impermanence, and love.

Lally 2 fell asleep, hatbrim crumpled on Cotton's shoulder. In his jacket the Temptations wailed.

Propped between his knees, the rifle bothered Cotton. He was too conscious of it. It was too tangible. Only a means to an end in camp, an implement such as a stirrup or a baseball bat, here, on this night, it took on a chill and oily identity of its own. It purported. He wished Teft had not brought the damn thing along. Even more vehemently he wished that they were back in their sacks and that yesterday had never been.

Beside him the sleeping boy stirred, mumbling protest. Lally 2 had returned in dreams to the carnage which had racked the cabin after lights out, to the trauma which had compelled a twelve-year-old to set out by himself through the piney woods. Now all six of them were on their way, over the same road, through the same towns, backtracking physically to the scene of that original horror. They were crazy as hell, Cotton assured himself, but great, too, he assured himself. He must quit swearing. He no longer needed it, nor did they. His mouth was sour, the residue of yesterday's nausea. He closed his eyes. In the gardens of God a unicorn sang, a hippogriff danced, and Goodenow vomited.

Teft tooled up Mingus Mountain. Tires squealed on hairpin turns, and the air near the stars was cold. Below them the Verde River cut a fertile and enormous trench, and downriver, deep in cottonwoods, lay old Camp Verde, where Crook had been commander. Many a redskin had bitten the dust for this valley.

Teft tooled them over Mingus Mountain. He drove like a demon, but all of them were driven. It had been unanimous.

They zigged and zagged down through Jerome, peopled once by fifteen thousand bodies, reduced now to fifty haunted souls. The mountain here resembled the bare abdomen of a woman, a dead, a mangled woman. In her, fathered by Phelps, Dodge, and Douglas, were a hundred miles of shafts, drifts, and stopes, and out of her, by pick, shovel, and caesarian section, a billion-dollar child of copper, gold, and silver had been blasted, stripped, and smelted. Down, down the pickup dropped, exhaust popping, over the ashes of Chinamen and miners, over the graves of whores and gamblers, away from the acid stink of greed and into the innocent night.

"Pull over," Cotton ordered. "They must be buttsprung back there."

When they were off the road, outside Clarkdale, and stopped, and when he hopped out to switch places, what he saw in back made him swallow a lump in his throat. Seated with his back to the cab, Shecker had his arms clasped around Goodenow who sat between his legs, while Goodenow's arms enfolded Lally 1, who sat between his legs with the buffalo head over his own. They had done it for warmth up on the mountain. From three radios

Jimmie Rodgers yodeled about peach-pickin' time in Georgia. They were sound asleep and snug as eggs in a carton. Cotton stood looking at them. He recalled a shot he had once seen on a TV science show for kids: a nest of eggs filmed just as the baby chicks were pecking their shells apart to be born and to see what the hell was going on outside, the eggs wobbling and beaks chip, chip, chipping, then tiny, interested eyes and wet, delicate heads. We've got to do this tonight, he told himself, this last thing. The greatest. But can we. Was our egg rotten. Or were we cracked in the nest. Something chipped at him. A sensation wet and delicate emerged. It might have been mercy. Yes, we will, he told the three asleep, inside himself. We will no matter what, I promise. We'll go home supermen, I swear to God. Angrily he swiped at his nose with a sleeve and whacked the side of the pickup hard.

"Wake up, dammit!" he cried. "Two of you in the cab—move it!"

If you wanted to be Apaches badly enough, the Director had consoled them, you could. If you wanted to avoid the humiliation of being low team on the totem pole of achievement, you might. It was up to you. And it was true, for no matter how awkward or irresolute you might be on first base or with a bow, camp custom granted you a second chance, there was another way you might hoist yourself by the seat of your own Levi's. You could raid. If, in the night, you could steal the trophy of any tribe higher in rank, it was yours until the next powwow, together with the name and rewards.

Initially there were many raids, particularly upon the trophies of the Apaches and the Sioux, hung in places of honor on cabin walls and guarded savagely —unsuccessful raids although the Navajo moved up a notch by bagging the bear head of the Comanches. Without warning, war-whoops startled the canyon out of sleep as attacks were launched and repelled with fists and firecrackers and pails of water and other campers stumbled from their cabins, yawning, to watch the fun. The counselors never interfered. Raiding was good for boys. It taught grit. Into character it built cunning.

The Bedwetters knew they would never need to defend their chamber pot, and also that they could never expect to climb the camp ladder by physical prowess. Disorganized but dutiful they entered the game, attempting a raid the second night. They aimed high. The Apaches had already beaten off one foray by the Cheyenne, and the camp was scarcely settled down again when the Bedwetters stripped to undershorts and barefooted through the ponderosa after the biggest prize of all: the head of the bull buffalo.

Of course they botched it. They had an advantage, for the Apaches, having unposted their guards after the Cheyenne raid, were sacked out in arrogance and snoring. As softly as they could, the Bedwetters slipped from the shadow of one pine to the next.

*Goodenow giggled once. Lally 2 tripped on a root
and fell flat. They reached the cabin of the enemy,
inched the screen door open. Teft and Shecker, the
strongest, were to go in first and lift the trophy down,
but they were clumsier than cub bears and for some
dumb reason Shecker had clipped his radio to the
elastic band of his skivs and somehow, in darkness
and nerves, turned it on. Music yammered.*

*They were tackled and captured instantly.
Dragged outdoors by the Apaches, the oldest and
largest boys in camp, they were roped to a pine trunk
while one of the victors brought the chamber pot
from their cabin. Goodenow began to cry. So did
everyone, even Cotton, everyone but Teft. The other
tribes came out in skivs and pajamas to observe and
laugh. It served the Bedwetters right. They were born
losers. And while they cried and the camp laughed,
placing the pot on the ground and taking trium-
phant turns, the Apaches urinated in it.*

They buzzed through Sedona, in the incredible
Technicolor country where so many Westerns were
filmed and stars like Henry Fonda and Glenn Ford
and James Stewart and John Wayne did so many
incredible deeds for the camera and a percentage of
the gross. Cotton had Teft pull over so that they
could switch places again. They put Lally 2 back in
the cab with Goodenow, but when Shecker, who
had toughed it out in the open both stints, volun-
teered to tough it out again, Cotton let him. The
improvement in Shecker in one summer had been
terrific.

Now their cause was hopeless. They could neither steal status nor win respect. They would never have watermelon for dessert, never take in a midweek movie. For the rest of the summer they were doomed by the establishment to be the Bedwetters, the dandiest collection of dings ever to be inflicted upon Box Canyon Boys Camp. The morning after the final indignity at the hands of the Apaches they refused to rise and shine, refused to face the jeers of the other tribes. When Wheaties could not budge them, he went to breakfast. Except for Lally 2, who withdrew under his bed, they huddled in the warmth of their bags, eyes closed, or lay on their backs looking at the ceiling, radios pulsing. The air in the cabin was oppressive with tension and dirty socks and despair and peepee.

Cotton lay thinking. Is this the time. What've I got to work with. A teeth-grinder. A head-banger. Two actual bedwetters. A nail-biter and overeater. And a thumb-sucker and bad-dreamer. And they all sleep with radios and talk in their sleep. I'm the only one normal out of six. I'm the only one who can do it. And if I don't now, it'll be too late. So get the lead out. Get the show on the road.

Feet on the floor, whistling to attract attention, he rummaged in his footlocker. In it were a few items he'd been saving just in case. Round his neck he put a set of army dogtags he had bought in a surplus store in Cleveland. They jingled. Teft and Goodenow were watching. Next he got out an electric razor, plugged it in, and ran it over his cheeks and chin. He was only fifteen and had little need to shave, but he had a razor ready against the day when. Now Shecker and Lally 1 were watching and the head of Lally 2 turtled from beneath his bed. Next, putting the razor away and rummaging further, he brought out a small cigar and one of the four two-ounce bottles of whiskey he'd bagged from the cart while the stewardesses were selling drinks on the plane coming out and having hernias trying to handle Teft, who'd run amuck. He sat down on his bed, broke the seal on the bottle, had a snort, then lit the cigar and puffed sufficient smoke. Their eyes bugged. He had them. This was the time.

Cotton laid it on the line. He told them the mess they'd made of last night's raid was the worst thing that had ever happened to him and he wanted no more of that and neither did they, he knew. Wheaties was off their backs and that was good, but if they wanted to get anywhere or be anybody this summer they had to have a leader who understood their problems but at the same time made them snap crap. He said he might as well be the one. If anyone wanted to fight him for it, he'd fight, but if not, he was taking over. Period.

"Okay, here's my first orders," he said. He had another snort and coughed and tried to blow a smoke ring and coughed but nobody smiled. "From now on none of us writes home or phones home. We're on our own. Our mothers and fathers can go to hell. Second, we call each other by our last names,

Lally 1, Goodenow, so on. Anybody calls me John Cotton gets a mouthful of teeth. Now my last order—get our cans out of bed and up to that chow cabin and don't bat an eye no matter what anybody says. Now move it."

They poured through Oak Creek Canyon like tea through a tin horn, then slowed to a crawl as Teft downshifted from drive to third to second and finally to low gear for the climb. They had reached the Mogollon Rim. It was a fault of earth, inconceivable and Paleozoic. It was the sheer limestone scarp at the southern jump-off of a plateau upheaved from sea bottom in the age of dinosaurs and armored fish and forming now vast areas of four of the United States. They must scale it. To and from and up along the wall the pickup labored, gulping oil and shuddering. From four thousand feet they climbed to five thousand and six thousand and seven thousand, and suddenly the air was rare and cold again and the truck gasped for it and gained speed and they were on top.

Shecker, Lally 1, and Cotton were in back, bundled together. After they had covered ten miles or so of tableland and forest, Cotton unwrapped himself from Lally 1, clamped the strap of his helmet liner under his chin so that it would not blow off, got onto his knees, and raised his head into the airstream above the cab.

The horizon shimmered. Behind it, black against a purple sky, were three cones familiar to him, the

San Franciscos, peaking at twelve thousand feet. But the dazzle along the horizon was what made him drop down and drum the cab window and point. Teft and Goodenow snapped to and Lally 2 woke up and peered ahead as Cotton, shouting, made mute syllables with his mouth:

"Flag-staff!"

7

I GOTTA EAT," SHECKER WHINED. "HOT PASTRAMI and a pickle and a strawberry shake."

"We're not stopping," Cotton said. "We don't have time and you know it."

"So am I starving," said Lally 1.

"My gut doesn't know it," Shecker said. "Me for food, glorious food." He climbed over the side of the bed and stood in the street, gnawing at a fingernail. "So go on without me and have fun."

"Me, too," said Lally 1. "You can't order us around all the time, Cotton."

Cotton was irate. They had stopped for a red light at the fringe of Flagstaff and now the light was green. "Get the hell back in here!"

"Up yours," Shecker said. "I've sat in back all the way, I should get something."

"We do what we want!" cried Lally 1.

As far as Cotton was concerned, that tied it. Teft and Goodenow had their heads out the cab window. "Okay, leave 'em!" he ordered Teft. "Go on, leave 'em!"

Teft obeyed, and the truck moved away and the mutineers began walking and none of them could quite believe what was happening, that the Bedwetters were breaking up, zap, pow, just like that, over nothing, when they were nearly there. But in less than a block Cotton pounded on the window and ordered Teft to pull over and in a minute Shecker and Lally 1 caught up with them. Cotton said okay, to get in, everybody was probably hungry and would operate better after some food, so get in and hit the floor while he looked for a place, there'd be a lot more fuzz in Flag than there had been in Prescott. He put Goodenow in back with them and slid in beside Lally 2 in the cab and they started again.

Intersecting with the main street, Teft turned right. This was U.S. 66, the central east-west conduit of the nation. In the good old days, guiding on a tall pine trimmed of boughs, known then as a flagstaff, wagon trains had watered at the springs here and bedded down for the night. Now the town was a day's run out of Los Angeles, and its main street, U.S. 66, was a caravansary of ten-dollar rooms, diesel spatter, clogged urinals, tubercular waitresses, anti-sleep pills, yesterday's pastry, flat tires, paper diapers, cigarette butts, and exhausted coffee, as tawdry by night as it was depressing by day. Cotton told Teft to turn off, away from the ratrace, and onto a side street. It was now 1:51 A.M.

Against a transient parental environment, which was overstimulating and unpredictable as well, Billy Lally's defense was to withdraw into a world of fantasy, self-created, into an isolation to which he admitted no one. His case was complicated by his discovery that the more completely he regressed, the greater advantage this gave him over Stephen, his older brother, so that withdrawal became for him both a necessity and a device. It was habitual now, with attendant infantile practices. Besides wetting his bed and sucking his thumb he had bad dreams and suffered night terrors. His parents twice enrolled him in special schools, only to take him out to travel with them. At various times he began treatment with four different therapists, one of them in Switzerland, only to have his father and mother reconcile and pack their suitcases. At twelve he was the youngest camper, and underage by restrictions, but his parents could not have gone to Kenya without disposing of both sons somewhere and the Director was persuaded to make an exception. Cotton's cabin was his second. When, in the first, he withdrew under his bed with the foamrubber pillow from home and curled into a ball in his sleeping bag, the other boys hauled him out, screaming as though ripped from the womb. He burrowed back in. They hauled him out again. The sport went on till Cotton came by and offered to take Billy Lally in with him. With him,

59

Cotton asserted, he could hide under his bed whenever he needed to, or up a tree, or in a cave for all he cared, or any damn where.

"Hold it," Cotton said. "Over there. Park and I'll make a recon."

He got out and crossed the dim street and spied into a yellow window, then returned and said to come on, this would do, and they piled out, leaving the engine running and stowing the rifle on the cab floor.

The place was an allnight beer and beanery with a griddle behind the counter and a mechanical bowling alley crowded between rickety chairs and tables. Two young men were drinking beer and bowling and on the floor, his head against the wall, an elderly Navajo snoozed in silver hair and a green velvet shirt. The Bedwetters lined up on stools and shortordered from the limited menu on the wall, two hamburgers each and a pint of milk. The counterman was bony and ketchupeyed and his chin had the contours of a spatula. On the wall beside the menu was this notice, flyspecked: "Our Credit Mgr. Is Helen Waite. If you Want Credit Go to Helen Waite." Balls trundled on the alley and pins clattered and bells rang, but when the game was over, the only sounds in the beanery were the hiss of grease and the caterwaul, issuing from two jacket pockets, of Grandpa Jones, and from three, of Gladys Knight and the Pips.

Glasses in hand, the two bowlers came up behind the six boys at the counter. They were young men of twenty or so in tight jeans and sassy western shirts and big belt buckles and long sideburns.

"What you milkdrinkers doin' out so late by your ownselves?" asked one.

Waiting for their hamburgers, the Bedwetters strawed milk from the cartons.

"How's come you listen to all them radios?" asked the other.

"We're musicians," Shecker said. "A rock outfit. Drums, four guitars, and a front singer. From L.A."

"Musicians, huh. You got a name?"

"Group Therapy," said Teft.

"Then we changed to After Death," said Goodenow, "but that was too morbid."

"So what're you now?"

"The Before Christ," Shecker said.

"Before Christ?"

"Dig our backs, man."

The sideburns studied the BC's on the backs of jackets. Then they studied the miscellany of headgear along the counter.

"Want an autographed picture?" asked Lally 1.

"Give us a listen on the Groovy label," said Goodenow.

The sideburns were not amused. "I asked what you doin' out so late," said one. "Now less hear, you hear?"

"In the West," said Teft, apropos of nothing in particular, "everything sticks, stings, or stinks."

"We're on tour," Shecker said. "Also we're talent scouts. Looking for local vocal talent."

"Sure," said Lally 1. "Sing something. We like it and we might wax you."

"We're from a boys' camp near Prescott," Cotton said quickly. "We've been camping out and now we're on our way back."

"Walkin'?"

"We've got a car."

The sideburns snorted. "None of you sonnys old enough to drive."

"You learn guitar and you might be as big as Simon and Garfunkel," Shecker said.

"Anything I can't abide," said one of the sideburns, reaching for Shecker's milk and pouring beer from his glass down the straw, "is a driplip dude kid."

"Would you like to know who my father is?" Shecker said.

"Okay." Cotton was off his stool. "Okay, you guys, let's go." He had his wallet out, and dropping a five on the counter, motioned at the door. "Let's go, we're late."

"But I'm hungry!" said Lally 2.

"I said let's go!" Cotton cried, his voice so shrill that it woke the Navajo in the green velvet shirt and the counterman dropped a plastic mustard dispenser and the other five were on the floor and ahead of him out the door like scalded cats.

"Walk, don't run," he said, his voice low now. "Walk and into that damn truck and let's roll, don't look back, act natural, and keep moving."

Just as they reached the pickup and were going

over the tailgate and into the cab the beanery door opened and the two locals stepped outside and watched as Teft cooled away from the curb.

"Why'd we have to leave?" demanded Goodenow, who was up front with Cotton. "What's the matter with those jerks?"

"Gunslingers," Cotton said. "Out for fun and games. And we can't take chances."

"Oh-oh," Teft said. He had turned left and intersected again with U.S. 66 and, waiting for a green light, stared into the big side mirror on the Chevy. "Trouble. I think it's them, the local Mafia."

"See if they tail us when we turn." The light changed and Teft swung onto the interstate. "They following?"

"Yup."

Cotton knocked on the cab window and yelled at those in back to lie low, then banged his helmet liner on the dash. "Dammit, to be almost there and run into those hoods and Shecker get funny in a New York accent. Anyway, stay in the speed limit till we're out of town, we can't afford to have the fuzz after us, too."

They snailed along at thirty-five for a mile, through a warren of motels and gas stations, then half a mile at forty-five, watching for the city limit sign. Cotton asked what kind of car the gunslingers were driving and Teft said a real rod, a '63 Plymouth he thought, which had been a hot model, and he could guess they'd souped it up—a pair of four-barrel carbs and a fullhouse cam at least, and chopped the front end. It would run rings around this thing.

"What do they want?" Goodenow asked faintly.

"To cut us down," Teft said. "Once we're out of town, pass and make us pull off."

"Then what?"

"Show us their talent."

"Talent?"

"Sure, sing for us."

Suddenly lights behind them blinked once, twice, three times, and a hardtop zoomed even with them and stayed even though Teft stepped on it, then drew slightly ahead and began to bear right, bearing down on the front fender of the pickup and offering two alternatives only: pull over or collide. Teft held course as long as he dared.

"Cotton," he said finally, "I've never done this before. I'm chicken."

"Pull over," Cotton said.

Goodenow put hands over his face. "What'll we ever, ever do?"

Teft braked gradually and left the highway and they chunked over gravel and came to a stop as the Plymouth crowded in close ahead of them and doused its lights. In their own lights they could see its wide, smooth tires, racing slicks, and extending from beneath it, puttering at them, four scavenger pipes.

The two locals strolled back toward the Chevy.

Even at second survey they did not seem mean or menacing. They were as clean and shaven and goodlooking, actually, as old Wheaties. But there was a scary difference. Old Wheaties was stupid. They were merely mindless. Wheaties had a lockerful of vices and a gizzardful of platitudes. They seemed to be unmotivated.

Cotton put the .22 on the cab floor and said to sit tight and stuck his head out the window and told the three in back to sit tight and no damn jokes.

"Well," said one local, "if it ain't The Before Christ. Howdy."

"Lights off," said the other.

Teft turned them off.

"Didn't eat your num-nums," said one.

"Everybody out," said the other.

Thumbs hooked in belts they waited on the highway side while the six boys climbed out and ranged themselves opposite, along the shoulder side of the pickup.

"How's come, if you're in a camp over to Prescott, you're headed for Albuquerque?" asked one.

No one answered.

"Less turn off that engine," said one sideburn, putting his head and arm into the cab. He ducked out. "I'll be a suckegg mule. No keys."

"Hey, you got this thing wired?" grinned the other.

"Whatta you guys want?" Cotton asked.

"Don't fuss now," one said, "Lessee what else."

He bent over the bed. "What the?" They both looked, then stood back grinning at the line of boys across the pickup, at their sober, stubborn faces as traffic passed. "If this ain't something to see in the night. Six milkdrinkers in a wired car and fancy hats with a half a pillow and a buffalo head with a bullethole in it."

"Whatta you want?" Cotton demanded.

One local scratched his head. "I dunno now."

"Me neither," said the other.

"Tell you what," said the first. "Less let the law know in Flag what we got here. They'd be obliged to hear about a wired car. Then they'd owe us a favor."

"You right," agreed the other. "You truly do have talent."

"Like to see something else?" Teft asked.

"Purely would."

Teft stood next to the cab. The door was open. Taking one step he was out of sight for five seconds. They heard a click. When he reappeared he laid the barrel of the rifle across the flanged top of the truck bed.

"You got a popgun," said one sideburn.

"Smile when you say that, stranger," Teft said.

"You wouldn't have the hair."

Teft took another step, backward, and turning, raised the .22, aimed, and fired. There was a high-pitched explosion after the rifle crack, then a lugubrious sigh, and the Plymouth settled perceptibly to the right. He had punctured one of the racing slicks. *They put him aboard the plane at Kennedy like a prisoner. His father pulled strings and boarded with him and guarded him till they detached the loading ramp from the aircraft. There were eighteen other boys aboard for the flight to Phoenix, and a dozen more were due to board when they landed at O'Hare in Chicago. No one was supposed to de-plane. Teft did, though. Service personnel caught him after a merry chase round and round the terminal and half walked, half carried him aboard again. The continuation to Phoenix was non-stop, and Teft made it a memorable flight for crew and passengers. After he tried to open an emergency exit at 35,000 feet, the first officer belted him into his seat, arms and all. Over Kansas the stewardesses allowed him to go to the john. On the way aft he flipped open an overhead hatch and ripped out an oxygen mask by the roots, providing an excuse for several grandmotherly females, who were convinced this would decompress the cabin and give them the bends, to have nervous breakdowns. In the john he locked the door and refused to come out. Before the first officer could force the "Occupied" lock with a screwdriver, Teft jammed the Kleenex and toilet paper and soap and towels down the head and ran water into the washbowl till the john floor was flooded. The crew belted him into a window seat and posted a stewardess. But as New Mexico appeared below him, he ceased to struggle and hunched forward, gazing open-mouthed. Lawrence Teft, III, was from Mamaroneck, New York. He had seen country like this in Westerns, but he had never believed the illimitable redrock land was real.*

None of them could comprehend it. Behind the barrier of the pickup the Bedwetters stood at attention like tin soldiers. Before the two locals could react, Teft ejected, chambered a second round, clicked the bolt home, laid the barrel of the rifle over the top of the bed again, leaned, sighted on them.

"I got the hair," Teft said, too loudly. "And I got another BB in here, And you start for Flag or I'll hang it in your ear. This close I can't miss. So start walking or one of you country & western hippies can wear earrings."

The sideburns stared at him.

"You hear me, hippies?" Teft shouted. "I said move—move it!"

"Partner, you gonna pay for this," said one.

But they did start, their boots crunching gravel, their figures enlarged by the sweep of headlights and diminished as darkness cut them down to size. When they were a hundred yards away, Cotton pushed the button.

"In the truck—fast! C'mon, let's roll!"

They jumped into the bed and the cab and Cotton grabbed the .22 from Teft and unloaded and as soon as the Chevy was geared up and hightailing down the interstate again they let loose.

"Yaaaaay, Teft!"

"What hair!"

"The Daltons ride again!"

"Earrings!"

"Nothing stops us!"

"Teft, goddammit, Teft, I can't tell you!" Cotton warbled. "But that was beautiful! Beautiful!"

8

"OH-OH."

A thought punctured. Cotton's exultation sighed from him. "They'll phone the cops in Flag," he worried, "and identify us and this junker. And the cops'll radio out here for the state police to set up a roadblock on us. That's what they do on TV. Then we've had it. Unless we make the turnoff first. How far to the turnoff?"

Teft said seven, eight miles at most.

"Then floor it."

"Floor it?" Teft made a Ferrari face and pulled down the bill of his Afrika Korps cap and knuckled the wheel. *Jawohl!*

They watched the speedometer. It hit 80 mph and held and over the hullabaloo of the engine and the whine of the tires Teft shouted this was it, this was the best the old clunker had in her, and unless they threw a rod she sounded good for seven miles. Along they barreled, fearful the three in back would be blown away, hypnotized by the grayriver of concrete pouring under them and the trucks and cars and U-hauls and campers flitting by like moths in the other lane.

Cotton clutched the .22.

Goodenow was petrified. His fingers worked at the Hopi headband as though unbeading it.

"Whooooeeee!" Teft hollered.

Shecker was thrown out of four cabins in two days. On the third, Cotton let him in, and on the fourth, regretted it. Shecker was as insufferable as his father, the famous Sid, whose indulged and overdominated mimic and victim he had become. He was the screech of chalk on slate. He was as loud and nervous and nosy and braggart as New York. He nibbled compulsively at his nails, he ate compulsively, he rattled off his father's routines compulsively, he was always "on." And eventually Cotton confronted him.

They took in just about anything in that cabin, Cotton said, but they had to draw a line. They wanted no more of his father's jokes, no more about the saloons he played or the shows he was on or who important he knew or how much money he made. In short, shape up or ship out. Shecker said he knew what they really meant. It was because he was Jewish. Cotton sighed and said no, it wasn't, and if there was one thing they didn't need around there, on top of everything else, it was a persecution complex. Shecker shouted they were Nazis. That burned Cotton. No, he said, they weren't. They had their own problems and merely wanted a little less yak and a little more peace and quiet in which to solve them. Shecker lost control. Why didn't they call this camp what it really was, he screamed, a concentration camp? If they wanted him out, why didn't they just build an oven and gas him? Cotton groaned and made the mistake of turning his back and Shecker jumped him. He was bigger and forty pounds fatter and soon had Cotton down and lay on him like a lump, pounding him till the others yanked them apart.

The incident cleared the air. Shecker settled down and began to be human. When he did lapse, being Miami Beach or putting on the persecution act, all they had to do was chorus "Gas 'im!" and he cut the comedy.

Large yellow letters against brown wood, the sign on the right side leaped into the headlights without warning. Teft braked and slewed onto gravel and then they were turned and through the open gate and away from full-house cams and mechanical bowling alleys and civilization and abruptly, marvelously, back into the night again and the West.

It was two thirty-six. They had left Box Canyon Boys Camp at eleven forty-eight and now, three hours and a bagged truck and some milk and a shoot-out later, they were practically there. The last three miles would be slow going, however, for this road, a dirt singletrack which dipped into gullies and dry washes, was so corduroy that the frame of the pickup chattered with vibration. The sensation here was one of breadth and elevation and the triviality of their vehicle, which, like some quadru-pedal insect, explored the brow of the sleeping earth, feeling with the antennae of its headlights for something edible and finding only scrub oak and salt cedar and the manzanita bush. To assert them-selves and their importance they turned radios up, producing a cacophony of "The Ten Command-ments of Love" by Peaches and Herb and "I Feel Like I'm Fixin' to Die" by Country Joe and the Fish.

They had descended into a dry wash and across a wooden bridge and were grinding over the far lip when the engine sputtered.

It was Shecker's lousy personality, though, that goaded the Bedwetters into their first feat. The fourth week of camp a movie played the Prescott drive-in which they wanted painfully to see. It was The Professionals, *staring Burt Lancaster and Lee Marvin. The Apaches got to go of course, they were top tribe, but the Bedwetters had as much chance of seeing it as they had of winning a ballgame. For three nights in a row Shecker, who was accustomed to having his own New York way, swore that after lights out he was taking off and hiking into town and going to the late show. He did not, naturally. But the third night Cotton could bear no more of his mouth. All right, he said, can it and we'll all go, the damn scoring system's unfair so we'll beat it. And they did. After Wheaties was asleep they dressed, slipped down to the corral, saddled up, led horses out of camp and rode the two miles to the drive-in entrance at the edge of Prescott. The manager wouldn't let them in at first, mounted, but it was a week night and the late show and there were only a few cars of neckers and after Shecker slipped him a twenty-dollar bill he sold them tickets. They rode in, tied horses to loudspeakers, bought popcorn and ice cream bars and hot dogs and corn chips and Cokes and enchiladas and sat down and enjoyed themselves totally. In the last reel the Camp Director drove in like a posse—the twofaced theater manager had probably phoned him—and made some uncharitable remarks about juvenile delinquency. But while he discoursed they took their sweet time mounting up and so contrived not to miss the ending. Back at camp, the Director warned them: pull a similar stunt and he'd expel them. The Bedwetters listened and looked at each other like Lancaster and Lee Marvin.*

Teft floored it and pumped the handchoke. The engine responded and they bumped another hundred yards but no further. It conked out again, this time with a last carburetor gasp. Front and back, the six just sat there.

"Don't anybody say it," Teft said.

No one did.

"Don't even think it."

But everyone was.

"Maybe the wire's come unclipped," he said, and getting out, went round to the front of the truck, raised the hood, and extracting a flashlight from his pocket, switched it on, and had a superfluous look. Switching it off, he returned it to his pocket and let the hood down slowly, ceremoniously.

Through the windshield Cotton and Goodenow stared at him. From the bed, Shecker and the Lally brothers stared at him.

As though onstage, Teft stood self-consciously in the headlights. On his cap the silver eagle glittered. He began with a vagabond grin. "How about that?" he appealed. "I just never noticed the gauge. Believe it or not, I've bagged cars before and driven them dry and no sweat. I just wired a fresh one."

He lost his grin. "Destroyed," he said. "This really destroys me."

He gave up. Spreading his long arms he flapped them against his long legs in contrition. He opened his jacket to expose his chest.

"So I now offer myself. As a human sacrifice to the Gas God."

And with a low bow and a martyred expression he draped himself over the white altar of the hood. "You may now cut out my heart," he said, "and eat it."

Suddenly the stage went dark. Teft vanished. Cotton had pushed the headlight knob. It was the most unfortunate thing he could have done. For the night came down upon them. They cowered before it, and before the implications of an empty tank.

Except for the ticking sounds of the engine cooling, they sat in a kind of stranded silence, hushed by the dark and this new, blabbering proof of their ineptitude.

"Oh, I am so sorry," Teft said. "I am just Christfully sorry."

9

SORRY? YOU'RE SORRY!" COTTON BLASTED. "ONE hell of a lot of good that does!"

Shecker and the Lally brothers jumped over the tailgate and Goodenow slid across the seat and out of the cab. But his lash cracked after them.

"Dings! Dings! Wheaties was right—we are dings! We can't do anything right and we've got no damn excuse for living and—"

He choked in midsentence. Curious, they gathered at the cab window. But he had merely gone into another of his catatonic fits. Cotton sat upright at the wheel, his jaw outthrust under the army helmet, one hand grafted to the gearshift as though he were driving the truck himself, as though by motive power of will and energy generated by rage

77

he could refuel it and propel it onward. *His mother had been married three times and divorced three times and was now keeping a man ten years younger than she. Her favorite among the four was her second husband, a rich, grandfatherly manufacturer of ball bearings, for it was his generous settlement upon their divorce which gave her the house in Rocky River and the membership in the Cleveland Yacht Club and made her wealthy in her own right. The manufacturer was certainly John Cotton's favorite, for he belonged to a fishing club in Quebec, and once, when John was ten, took mother and son up there after trout. They flew in from North Bay, Ontario, by float plane and landed on the lake near the cabin. The next morning John and his stepfather went fishing, the boy trolling with a Daredevil, the man paddling the canoe. One after another the boy fought and netted Quebec reds, brook trout so-called because the coffee color of the water stained their undersides a vivid crimson. They drifted near a cow moose and her calf breakfasting on lilypads. It was a serene and thrilling morning. This was the best place he'd ever been, the boy blurted suddenly, and the best time he'd ever had, and he wished it would never end.*

His stepfather smiled. "You're a jimdandy, Johnny. I wish I could keep you."

"Will you and her get divorced?" the boy asked.

"Probably. She needs a younger man. And money even more, her own money."

"I wish you wouldn't."

With the paddle his stepfather carved deep into the black of the lake. "Perhaps she'd sell you to me."

"She prob'ly would," the boy said.

When they returned to the cabin his mother, already bored with Quebec, wanted to fly back to Cleveland in the morning. Her son and husband objected. She made a scene and won.

That night ten-year-old John Cotton took a hammer and an awl, swam naked through icy water to the plane moored offshore, held his breath, ducked, and hammered a hole in the bottom of a float.

In the morning the plane lay over on one wingtip. The pilot had to hike through the bush to Deux Rivières and phone North Bay for a mechanic. It required three days to make repairs and John Cotton caught another thirty-one trout. Knowing they could not have pried him loose from the steering wheel and gearshift with a crowbar, the five outside the cab turned away until he was released from seizure.

When he was, when he had come to, the Bedwetters were already isolating. What had been, only minutes before, a functioning unit, had become a rabble. They blew about the pickup like tumbleweeds. Nomads in a wilderness of doubt, hither and yon they strayed, reabsorbed in self, their cause forgotten, each one tending the petty flock of his own anxieties. Cotton could have tied knots with their tensions. Had he been joker enough to honk the horn, they would have taken off for the moon like bigassed birds, sent into gabbling orbit. He listened to them. Here we go again, he sighed, gathering nuts in the night.

"I'm tired," said smaller cowboy hat, pillow under its arm and thumb in its mouth. "After all, I'm the youngest."

Arnold Palmer's golf cap was taking a leak into a manzanita bush. "Geez, I'm dying of malnutrition," it said. "We should've ordered those hamburgers to go. So it shouldn't have been a total loss."

"I'm hungrier than anybody," whined the Hopi headband. "You guys at least had supper and I lost mine."

The Afrika Korps maneuvered in circles around the truck. "I got us wheels and I drove us. Why do I have to be responsible for gas, too?"

"I didn't wanna come on this in the first place," griped the bigger cowboy hat. "Just because I'm stuck with a psycho brother."

"I miss the tube," said the smaller cowboy hat, ignoring bigger. "It's not healthy for you to go without TV too long."

"I wish I was in Vegas right now," said golf cap, buttoning up. "They cut the steaks special for my father in Vegas."

"When I get home," resolved the bigger cowboy hat, "I want a whole week tube time. Got my own color set."

"Hey, didn't I rupture that tire, though? Poom!" boasted Rommel. "How come I can't score on the range?"

"There's one show I like," admitted Hopi head-band. "Because the guy's only got a little while to live. He might die any show. I'm sort of morbid that way."

They wearied, they sickened, they gave Cotton a royal pain in the rear. Okay, he said to himself, okay, let's just see. Let's turn off the damn set and see if they can survive on the real thing. Let's stick the horse opera back in the can and see if they're grown-up enough to live in this world. If they aren't, if they poop out now, the hell with the whole operation and the hell with them, too, because if they aren't, after this summer and all I've done for them, they really are born losers, they really are dings. But if they can, if they'll at least try to hack it without me, then they're over the rim, they've won the big game, and when they fly home they'll be okay, they can hack anything, even home.

He left the cab. Going round to the front end of the truck he took off his helmet and cocked a boot up on the bumper. Automatically the squad assem-bled and hunkered down around him quietly, as they had earlier, in the piney woods.

"I lay it on the line," he said. "Running out of gas wasn't Teft's fault, it was everybody's. But it really louses up the operation." They had only a mile more to go, he said, but now, with no wheels, they had to think about afterwards and consequences. There were two options. Hike back to U.S. 66, hitch a ride into Flag, wire another car and rod back to Prescott and the horses and they'd probably be back in camp and in bed before daylight. No one would know. No one would ever connect them. But go on, carry the thing through and lose that time and they'd surely hit camp in broad daylight, the Director would third-degree them about where they'd been and even if they clammed up, when what they'd pulled off made the newspapers he'd smell a rat—the stolen pickup in Prescott, abandoned out here, the locals in Flagstaff who'd identify it and them—and the Bedwetters would be in trouble, legitimate trouble, with the camp and the law and their folks. So that was it. Head for home now and maybe make it in time or go on and sure as hell get caught and was it worth it?

"So we're gonna vote again," he said. "I told you, I won't be head honcho this time. But before we vote, I want to say something you maybe haven't thought of. Sure, I know what we saw today—I mean yesterday. I know what it did to us. And we think tonight's something we have to do, or we wouldn't be here. But if we think it'll make us heroes or any movie junk like that—it won't. No one else will give a damn but us. In fact, it'll make a lot of people mad enough to shoot us. So what I'm saying is, it doesn't matter to anybody but us. And in three days, don't forget, we break up, camp's over. We'll prob'ly never see each other again."

He dropped his boot. "Okay, we vote. Everybody's gotta be in favor. All in favor of skipping the whole crazy deal and heading for camp and keeping our noses clean, raise your right hand."

Instantly he raised his right hand.

He could not see their faces, but the effect upon them, the shock, was almost palpable. He kept his hand high. No one spoke, no one moved.

"Cotton, you flake-out!"

It was Lally 2, on his feet, throwing down his pillow. "I was going alone till you talked me out of it—now you get us here and flake out yourself!"

"Go find a bed," his brother sneered. "Crawl under the truck."

"You shut up. Let's take another vote—all in favor of going on like we said no matter what!" Lally 2 raised his right hand.

The other four were whipsawed. Under the two hands they squatted, contemplating their hangups and the rutted road beneath them.

Lally 2 lowered his hand. Scornfully he picked up the chared pillow, scornfully dusted it off. "What a bunch of dings," he said. "You can't do anything without Cotton any more. What'll you do when you get home and he's not around?" Tucking pillow under arm, he jerked the cowboy hat firmly over his ears. "Well, I don't need anybody. I started out by my own self and I'm still going and if anybody wants to tag along, they can."

And away he went, into the dark, down the road as obdurately as he had the road through the piney woods. Cotton's arm was still high, and tiring. He began to sweat. One gone, he thought, and five to go.

"Wait a sec," Goodenow called after Lally 2.

"What?"

"Would you help carry the head?"

"I might."

Goodenow moved to the truck bed and came back lugging the buffalo head and horns. "I'm sorry, Cotton," he said, "but he's too little to go by himself."

Lally 1 spat. "Judas Priest, why'd you have to say that? Now I have to go. Anything happened to him, our folks'd cut me down. You wouldn't believe the way they baby him."

He joined Goodenow and together they trudged off.

"Hey, you hear the one about the three storks?" Shecker asked, standing and rubbing his hands preparatory to a monologue. "The mama stork asked the papa stork what he'd done that day and he said, delivered triplets. He asked what she'd done and she said, delivered twins. So the mama and papa stork asked the baby stork what he'd done and he said, not much but he sure scared hell out of a couple of teenagers." He bit a cuticle. "Like the man says, when ya gotta go, ya gotta go." He rocked back and forth on his heels. "Well, see you in the papers. Or jail, heh-heh."

When he had gone, Cotton lowered his hand. Teft unwound himself, simulated a yawn, faked a stretch, lifted the truck hood, unclipped his hotwire, coiled it into a pocket, dropped the hood, loitered to the cab, eased out the rifle, and lazed back to Cotton.

"So long, partner," he declaimed in his finest last-reel, into-the-sunset drawl. "We've rode many a mile together, but now I reckon we've opened us two differ'nt cans of peaches." Head bowed, he flicked away an onion tear. *"Auf wiedersehen."*

An about-face and he left Cotton alone by the truck, tramping down the road tilted a little on the rifle side, dissolving at length into mist. For a thorn of loss pierced Cotton, and his eyes misted. It was true: they no longer needed him. Standing there, he combed a hand through his red, matted hair. But after the pain a vast, ripe grape of joy burst in him and he had to hold on to keep from bounding after them, whooping and hollering, I didn't mean it, I wasn't flaking out, I was just putting you over a barrel to see what you'd do and now I know! You're great, you guys, great! Now we really can hack it, we can hack anything—because you finally don't need me or anybody any more! We're finally honest-to-God committed to something better than that peepot and we did it ourselves! So let's go, goddammit, come hell or high water or camp or the fuzz or our folks or the Viet Cong, let's go! Instead, he clapped on his helmet and took out after the troops. He marched, he did not run, counting a slow, dignified cadence and fighting down an undignified impulse to whistle. In a minute or two he picked them up by the white BC's on their jackets.

He kept going, between and among them, and they cleared their throats in greeting and relief and closed ranks around him and had the grace, for which he was thankful, to leave everything obvious unsaid. But he was embarrassed and so were they and after a while he broke it. Step it up, he said sergeantly, get the lead out. Hup, hup, hup.

10

S MARTLY THEY STEPPED OUT, FULL OF BEANS AGAIN.
But in a quarter-mile they halted in consternation.
What halted them was the sound of their boots,
scuffing, magnified—that sound and no other.

For there was no other now. Out of pockets they
hauled radios, thumping them and twiddling the
controls, to no avail. Every station had gone off the
air, every adenoid and A-string. They were orphaned.

To divert them from this low, appalling blow,
Cotton flashed his wrist. It was 3.02 in the A.M.
Okay, he whispered, they must be nearly there, so
no lights from here on out, no chatter or horsing
around, and keep close together.

This last was unnecessary. When he took the
point, leading them, they ganged up behind, stum-

87

bling over his heels as he slowed and they slowed. Step by step they were turned from volunteers into conscripts. It was more than the loss of communication. In the cold and stillness at seven thousand feet they seemed skinny to themselves, and younger, and more vulnerable. And the presage of the night had changed. For three hours, through woods and towns and over mountains, they had been Godsped on their journey by the moon. It failed them now. It lay down in the west among some aged, August stars. A grumble of clouds blacked it out at intervals. Off the road and on again the Bedwetters yawed, directed this way and that by a senile breeze. They tripped on a secret. Weather might be born elsewhere, it occurred to them, weather might have its way with boys and nations elsewhere, but up here, on this plateau, at this lonesome elevation, it grew old and addled and weak. Up here, on the bald pate of Arizona, weather kicked the bucket.

Then they were given a cloud gap, and good light. They were there. Another fifty yards and they would blunder into a closed gate. Beyond the gate the dirt road curved past the campground with its motor pool of vehicles, cars and campers and trailers and pickups and jeeps and refrigerator trucks, past smoldering fires, past the tents pitched by those who chose not to sleep in their cars, past the skinning shed and ranchhouse of stone and on into the range. The vehicles were more numerous than they had seemed yesterday, and the small army of lust and murder and indifference which, if aroused, would oppose them, seemed more formidable.

Cotton held them at the gate. Beyond was the fenced lane to the pens and the killing ground where, in his dream, Goodenow had fallen first, then Lally 2, enclosed by the wire into which he had hurled himself before he recognized his mother's face and her bullet broke his brain.

He held them until the moon was obscured. Then they climbed the gate, handing over rifle and pillow and head and horns, and left the road to cross the killing ground.

Suddenly the earth was treacherous underboot. They slipped and reeled. Goodenow fell. Balancing, they waited for him to rise, but he did not. Instead, he began to retch. On hands and knees he was paralyzed by a series of dry, ghastly heaves. *Goodenow threatened suicide a second time after Cotton caught him telephoning his mother one night and wrestled the phone away and cut the connection. Goodenow burst into tears, which he did on the slightest excuse. Cotton reminded him of his original orders: no calls or letters home. Blubbering he was going to hang himself, Goodenow rushed off through the dark toward the tack barn. "Go bead a belt," Cotton said disgustedly, recalling how the sissy had stood chin-deep in the tank all day making a fool of himself, and let him go. Ten minutes later, on second thought and also because they were both from Ohio, he went to the barn, to find Goodenow standing on a feed bin with a rope over a rafter and a noose around his neck, ready to jump. Cotton was up half the night convincing Goodenow of the wisdom and equity of his rule. If they were ever to act their age, and Goodenow was fourteen, if they were ever to stand on their hind legs and spit life in the eye, they must begin now, this summer. Goodenow came down from the feed bin finally, and on the way back to bed he told Cotton about a thing they had done in the special school he'd gone to in Shaker Heights. "Bumping," it was called. When everybody was about to crash and burn and needed help, fast, the teacher would have them huddle and close eyes and hug each other and touch each other for a minute, and it really worked. Goodenow said he could use a little bumping once in a while, all of them could, and Cotton said okay, they'd try it. He never knew whether Goodenow would actually have hung himself or not.*

They were unable to get Goodenow off his hands and knees, and he was too convulsed by retching to tell them what was wrong. They knelt about him to help, but in so doing touched earth with their own hands and instantly, reflexively, withdrew them. They had been walking in, had put hands upon, something wet and cold and viscid. They tried to cleanse hands on jackets and jeans but could not. They tried to rise and run away, but slipping, sliding, could not. They wallowed. They were like children making terrible mudpies.

Then the shutter of cloud opened. They saw.

They knew. In a lens of unnatural light the Bed-wetters posed, kneeling, squatting, sitting in a grotesque of horror, faces contorted, several groaning, all six of them in stasis. One click of moonlight exposed the game and ended the adventure. One look shrieked what it was that smeared their palms and pants and chins and boots. It was blood.

BUFFALO PRESERVE

ARIZONA GAME AND FISH DEPARTMENT

ROSCOE RANCH   4 MILES SOUTH

VISITORS WELCOME

THIS WAS THE YELLOW LETTERING ON A BIG BROWN
sign alongside U.S. 66 eight miles east of Flagstaff.
They had seen it from the pickup early yesterday
morning while headed back to Box Canyon Boys
Camp after an overnight campout in the Petrified
Forest. Wheaties was driving, two boys beside him
in the cab and the other four in the bed with
sleeping bags and gear.

The Bedwetters had the idea simultaneously.
Those in back hammered on the cab window, the

two in front argued they were not due in camp till afternoon anyway, this might be the only chance they would ever have to see a herd of real buffalo, and after a mile or two of debate, Wheaties gave in, chauffeuring them back to the sign and through the gate and down the dirt road across the plateau.

They stopped at a closed gate. The road on the other side continued past a ranchhouse and a motley of vehicles, most of them parked side by side to form a barricade, and a small army of men, women, and children sat on hoods or fenders or bumpers, waiting. There were horsemen near the gate, mounted, waiting.

They opened the gate, passed through, closed it, and drove down the road. Wheaties pulled the pickup into line with the other vehicles. Here they faced an acre of open ground, barren except for dark spillings. The acre was wire-fenced on its opposite side, and a fenced lane led away past a little pond. Ten yards in front of the barricade of cars and pickups and campers, a tarpaulin had been spread. On it, a heavy rifle with a telescopic sight in her lap, a young woman in jeans sat waiting.

The young visitors waited, too. It was a vivid morning. Sun glanced from metal. The high, dry air was crystalline with suspense.

Then men, women, and children murmured. Down the lane bobbed three brown, four-legged shapes, three toy animals in the distance. Lingering at the little pond to drink, they were driven on into the open ground by other horsemen, waving hats and shouting.

They paused together, a bull and two cows, fullgrown, confronting the barricade of vehicles and humans. Curious, they tossed their heads. These were semidomesticated buffalo, from four to ten years old. Born on this preserve, fear of men had been bred out of them. Inoculated against disease, they were prime. Fed hay when winter snows covered their browse, they followed a feed truck about like sheep. They had never known the arrow or the lance, the lightning or the fire which crazed their ancestors over cliffs and into swollen rivers, nor had they known, until yesterday, the sound and implication of a gun.

Now the range between the young woman on the tarpaulin and the three buffalo was less than a hundred yards. She raised the rifle, notching it between her knees, and sighted on the bull. She fired. Dust exploded on the hillside beyond the fence and the three animals exploded into a headlong run toward the main gate. Their speed was incredible. Turned near the gate by riders who galloped after them, they stampeded around the ranchhouse and into the killing ground again, where other horsemen barred their way.

Ashamed of her marksmanship, the young woman buried her face in her hands. Under her shirt, taut over the shoulders, her body quivered. But as the animals gathered again, stamping, winded by their run, she lifted her head, sighted, and fired. Dust flew from the bull's hide. He leaped straight up, clearing the ground with all four hooves, and dropping, was hit a second time and a third. Still he did not go down. He was massive, he was beautiful, he stood as though made of marble to adorn and fill a fountain of the Renaissance. He lowered head and horns in resignation, extended a thick gray tongue, and suddenly, luridly, from his open mouth a gush of liquid crimson issued, and as he breathed, bubbles of crimson formed about his nostrils, dilating, glazed in sunlight, until they burst in froth. At this first offering of blood a long sigh went up from men and women and children waiting, a tremulous amen of pleasure.

The young woman fired two more rounds into the bull. He toppled. Applause spattered. Horns honked. Weapon high in victory, she sprang to her feet. Her cheeks were bright with tears. Her face was inspired by a discovery almost carnal.

A grayhaired man in his sixties, a physician, it was said, took her place on the tarpaulin immediately, and knelt, and sighted. For the two cows seemed to present themselves as targets. They stood beside the bull as though in sorrow, nosing his hump and head and snuffing an odor alien to them. The physician fired. He hit the larger cow in the belly. Her legs stiffened. Arching her tail, she evacuated her bowels. He fired again and she went down, only to rise to meet another bullet. Twice she fell, twice she lurched upright, shaking her head, hide twitching. But she did not bleed. When she foundered at last, her four legs doubled and extended for several minutes as though she were running lying down, running from death in life.

The remaining animal ran for her life, around the barricade of vehicles, horsemen in pursuit, past the skinning shed, circling the ranchhouse to be opposed by other horsemen, who harried her again to the killing ground.

The third shooter was called. A boy of fourteen or fifteen threw himself clumsily into the prone position on the canvas. There were shouts of advice —to fire away, to hit 'er in the ear, to hold his water and take his time. The boy's rifle seemed as long as he was. It wavered on the prop of his forearms. And he was overeager, firing before properly sighted. He missed, and terrorized, the cow plunged away to race a second complete circuit of the ranchhouse. Driven again to a place near the carcasses of bull and cow, she was entirely winded. Her head sagged, her eyes bulged, her tongue lolled from her mouth to touch the ground. The boy fired. Her hindquarters folded under her, so that she sat up on rigid forelegs. It unnerved the boy. He began to fire round after round. At the impact of the fifth, miraculously the animal heaved herself up and lunging for the wire fence behind her, tried to leap it. She crashed on top and bore it half down under her bulk, forelegs on one side and hind on the other, crabbing, helpless as some sea mammal caught high and dry by a tide, snorting agony as the boy, reloading, put bullets into her until blood was pumped in gouts from her ears and mouth and from beneath her tail.

Over the impending ceremony he had night sweats for weeks. He lost no weight, however, because he ate to compensate. You could buy or borrow a canned speech, but his father, Sid, insisted on writing one himself, with help from his writers—then put it off until so late that Sammy had insufficient time to memorize. The morning of bar mitzvah *came. They left the townhouse on Sixty-Fourth Street for the synagogue. Six hundred people were waiting, more than half of them Sid's big-name show-biz friends. There would be a thousand in the Hotel Taft for the feasting that night, which would cost Sid, he was avid to reveal, ten G's. Sammy read in Hebrew from the* Torah *and* Haftarah *and the rabbi made a few remarks of welcome. Then, dressed in a new suit, Sammy took his place at the lectern and began. "My dear rabbi, wonderful parents, family, and friends. On this, the most important day of my life, I have been honored by your presence. And as I look ahead to my manhood, I will cherish your good wishes and fine thoughts. You have given me the strength, the support, the support . . ." He forgot. He could remember nothing. He went wet all over. His father's face was livid. His mother bowed her head. Instinctively Sammy did one of his father's*

97

*jokes about the two Gentiles vacationing at Mi-
ami Beach. There was no laughter at the punch-
line. In extremity he rushed on, beginning the
one about the Jew who stowed away aboard the
Mayflower before Sid Shecker reached him.*

What the young visitors had happened upon was
the second day of the annual three-day "hunt"
staged and supervised by the Arizona Game and
Fish Department. Of the sixty million buffalo
estimated to range the American West a century
ago, there remained but a few thousand now,
surviving in small herds which were confined to
preserves and managed either by the various states
or by the federal government. To maintain a scien-
tific ratio between the natural increase in numbers
of animals and the limited areas available for their
exclusive habitat, it was necessary to "thin" or
"harvest" each herd periodically. The two herds in
Arizona, one on the Kaibab, north of the Grand
Canyon, and this one, near Flagstaff, were reduced
in alternate years from 250 to approximately 150
"head" of healthy, calf-producing cows and sufficient bulls. Ninety were being harvested this summer, thirty a day for three days, by Arizona
sportsmen.

It was not called a "hunt." The hunters were
referred to as "shooters." There were invariably
more shooters than buffalo to satisfy them. Several
hundred applied by mail each year for a permit,
enclosing a check for forty dollars. A drawing was

held, and the first ninety applications drawn were granted permits and divided into three groups, one for each day. The lucky ones were instructed where and when to report and informed that, while most of the meat would be distributed among the kitchens of state institutions, for their forty dollars they would be allowed to keep for personal use the head, hide, a forequarter, and the heart and liver of their kill. On the day appointed, the permit holders' names were called in the order in which they had been drawn. Three animals were released from the pens each half hour, and the shooting began.

On this day, the second, the first three buffalo were now dead. After the shooters had walked out to admire their trophies, the carcasses were hoisted into the bed of a pickup with a tripod winch, driven to the skinning shed, hoisted again by means of windup winches and cables attached to rear ankles, and three teams of rubber-aproned skinners went to work with knives and electric saws. By this time another shooter was ready on the tarpaulin, the horsemen were positioned, and three more head were shouted from the pens.

To kill thirty buffalo required between six and seven hours. At that close range, a single round in the ear would have ended an animal as instantly and humanely as cattle were destroyed by packing companies, but male or female, old or young, skilled marksmen or weekend shotgunners, strange things happened to Americans when they attempted to fix in their sights the most American of all species. Shooting from less than a hundred yards at enormous stationary targets, firing heavy .30–06 and .30–30 caliber weapons, they were somehow emotionally or psychically incapable of killing well.

They gutshot.

They blasted horns from heads.

They blinded.

They crippled, shattering hocks and fetlocks.

They bled buffalo to death before striking a vital organ.

They enfiladed the killing ground with fire as pitiless as it was futile.

A festive atmosphere developed. The hunt became at once a school picnic, a revival meeting, a civic barbecue, a patriotic ceremony, and a carnival of slaughter. Every sense of sight, hearing, smell, and decency was overwhelmed. The pure air, rent by explosion and echo, grew foul with powder. Victory horns bugled. Car radios brayed music and commercials. Cenotaphs of beer cans were erected. Children romped about to glean the bullet casings. Electric saws screamed through bone and the floor of the skinning shed ran red.

Dripping, still warm, forequarters were brought to the refrigerator trucks. The thickness of hump steaks was specified. Deposits on lockers were made.

Beyond the meat, nothing was wasted. Heads were to be mounted, hooves made into ashtrays, tails into fly-whisks, hides into auto robes. A distinctive coin purse, it was learned, could be fashioned from the scrotum of a bull.

And one by one, driven to exhaustion, trapped by fence and horses and bewilderment, under an immaculate sky the mythic creatures died. They died not in mercy, not in the majesty which was their due, but as the least of life, accursed of nature. They died in the dust of insult and the spittle of lead.

There was more here than profaned the eye or ear or nose or heart. There was more here than mere destruction. The American soul itself was involved, its anthropology.

We are born with buffalo blood upon our hands. In the prehistory of us all, the atavistic beasts appear. They graze the plains of our subconscious, they trample through our sleep, and in our dreams we cry out our damnation. We know what we have done, we violent people. We know that no species was created to exterminate another, and the sight of their remnant stirs in us the most profound lust, the most undying hatred, the most inexpiable guilt. A living buffalo mocks us. It has no place or purpose. It is a misbegotten child, a monster with which we cannot live and which we cannot live without. Therefore we slay, and slay again, for while a single buffalo remains, the sin of our fathers, and hence our own, is imperfect. But the slaughter of the buffalo is part of something larger. It is as though the land of Canaan into which we were led was too divine, and until we have done it every violence, until we have despoiled and murdered and dirtied every blessing, until we have erased every reminder of our original rape, until we have washed our hands of the blood of every other, we shall be unappeased. It is as though we are too proud to be beholden to Him. We cannot bear the goodness of God.

12

FROM INFANCY, STEPHEN AND BILLY LALLY WERE *contestants for the affection of their parents. Like lapdogs they barked and begged for tidbits tossed now to one, now fingerfed to the other. If one sibling learned a trick, such as regression, and was rewarded, the other learned to do a different trick. This is what the Lally brothers got for Christmas when Stephen was eleven, Billy nine: identical toy tanks and supporting armament; identical space suits and helmets; identical arrays of indoor and outdoor games; identical spincast rods and reels; identical cowboy costumes complete with six-shooters, hats, and boots; identical portable record players; identical swim fins and snorkels; identical assortments of Dinky toy sports cars; identical extra equipment for their identical electric trains; and identical racing bikes, except that one was red, one gold. Then their father and mother went off to an eggnog party. Stephen got the red bike but wanted the gold. Billy would not trade. On his parents' return, Stephen had a temper tantrum, screaming and rocking and butting his head against the wall. To console him, his mother promised to exchange the red bike for a gold and his father flew the family to Aspen to ski. After that, their parents left them with the butler, the maids, the chauffeur, the cook, and a governess, to winter in Morocco.*

After the first buffalo had been killed, they told Wheaties they were ready to go, they had seen enough. After the second, they insisted. After the third, they implored. He laughed at them. In a pig's ear he'd go. It was their idea, not his. They'd talked him into driving them all over Coconino County to see some real buffalo, it was the only chance they'd ever have—well, he had, they had, and if they didn't like it, they could lump it. He did. He thought it about the best thing he'd ever bumped into, better than a three-ring circus, and he intended to stay till every damn one of those buff was full of lead and skinned.

At the noon break they were unable to eat. Wheaties gobbled the stale food leftover from the camp-out.

Not until midafternoon and the last animal had gone down in beer and agony did they start for Box Canyon Boys Camp. They refused to sit in the cab with their junior counselor. The six rode in the truck bed, huddled speechless and grayfaced among the rolled sleeping bags. The journey seemed endless to them, through Flagstaff and Jerome and over Mingus Mountain and finally, as they paused for a stoplight by the courthouse in Prescott, Lally 2, the youngest, broke the seal of nausea.

"How many's still left?"

They knew what he meant.

"Thirty," Teft said. "For tomorrow."

"Where do they keep 'em?"

"Down in those pens," Shecker said.

They went on to camp, into the sighing ponderosa and the whoopdedo of the other boys, but they had nothing to say to anyone, they kept to themselves. After unloading the truck they went directly to the corral to care for their horses, currying them and feeding them and talking to them and dallying until the supper gong clanged. It was as though they could not abide the company of humans.

Lawrence Teft, III, was the loudest tooth-grinder of the lot. Cotton listened to him many a night, surprised he did not abrade them from their sockets, wondering what savage inner strife the habit manifested. Teft cried out much, too, in his sleep, the protestations vehement and garbled. When he was twelve he stole his mother's purse. It wasn't money, he had a liberal allowance. He could or would give no reason. Last year, when he was thirteen, he went one night for a jaunt in his father's Imperial, driving from Mamaroneck to White Plains, where, at an interchange on the Westchester Expressway, he collided with two other cars. Again he could or would not explain his motive, standing mute, hands in pockets, smiling that oblique, tilted smile. His father paid the damages and was at pains to see that his cars were thereafter garaged without keys. Two months later Lawrence Teft, III, hotwired and stole a neighbor's car. When it ran out of gas in Queens, he stole another. The police picked him up in a third car on the New Jersey Turnpike near Elizabeth at noon the next day. He was booked for speeding, reckless driving, driving without a license, and grand theft, vehicle, the latter charge reduced to joyriding. To unravel the escapade and keep it out of the newspapers and juvenile courts required three weeks and considerable expense, but his father was a general partner in an investment house in Wall Street.

No sooner had they finished supper, forcing food down, and stepped out of the chow cabin, when Goodenow puked. Later, until lights out, they wandered alone among the pines, strangers to each other, ashamed of themselves and of their kind.

It had been five minutes of eleven by his wrist when Cotton woke from his bad dream. Listening for radios, counting four, not five, and finding the sleeping bag under the bed unoccupied, he roused the Bedwetters with the news that Lally 2 was gone.

13

THEY WALLOWED.

For a stricken minute more in the blood and mud they tried to stand, gagging, and to assist the helpless Goodenow. Finally, hauling him by a wrist, they were able to crawl to dry sand and get him on his feet and stagger from the killing ground to the small pond, where they flopped and rubbed hands underwater, making cups of them and splashing filth from their chins and scrubbing it from knees and elbows.

They sat another minute, their hands and faces dripping. Nothing stirred about the ranchhouse or among the vehicles and tents. The next day's shooters slept well. From far out on the preserve an eerie requiem went up, and they got goosebumps. It was coyotes, howling soul.

Cotton started them along the fenced lane down which the meat was shooed from the pens, but moving slowly, almost reluctantly. It was well after three in the A.M.

The Bedwetters had never had a real plan, only a simple objective: no matter who, no matter what, to free from the pens the thirty animals doomed to die in the morning. But the fact was, none of them knew what the "pens" were. They had assumed some kind of enclosure like a corral, with a gate which had only to be opened. It could not be this gate, they realized, approaching the end of the lane. That would merely let the herd onto the killing ground, where it could be mowed down. There must be another gate, on the far side of the pens, through which they had been rounded up before the hunt. Opening that one would free them to scatter again over the range, reprieved from execution for two years. But finding that gate, and getting the prisoners through it, they now recognized, might be about as easy as playing ice hockey in hell.

They groped for the gate. They stopped dead in their tracks. They heard it, smelled it, felt it. They were in the presence of great beasts.

It was very dark. They could see nothing between the bars. But they heard snortings and stompings and in their nostrils was an odor rank and fierce and primal and suddenly, with a rumble and roar, something the size of a dinosaur came at them and a hot breath slapped their faces and they tumbled backward, barking shins and dropping the head and horns and tripping over the .22. One of the bulls had rushed them.

Cotton swore a soft blue streak and said to get out of there fast, and helping each other, slinging up the trophy and rifle and burnt, bloody pillow, they creaked up and over the wire fence and out of the lane, then up and over a second, and jumped down and stood around shaking till he said to come on, they were safe now.

They investigated the pens. The sides were eight feet high, the crossbars roughcut 4-by-8's as big as railroad ties which were bolted to posts a foot or more in diameter. Nothing less, evidently, would confine what was inside. There was no gate here.

They turned a corner. This was the long side of the rectangle, and it fronted the open range. They passed a Ford pickup with lettering and an insignia on its door, and a stack of baled hay. Cotton said they could talk now if they kept it down, they were far enough away from the ranch and the mighty hunters, but they couldn't goof around all night, they had to find the layout of the pens, so he was going up, right by this gate.

He climbed three bars high and got a cloud break and motioned the others up beside him. At first, on their toes, they peered out over what seemed a maze of pens, but as their eyes adjusted they could see that the entire rectangle was divided by inner walls into at least four smaller rectangles, and that the herd had to be in the far right corner section, facing the gate and lane. Along the tops of the inner walls, constructed of the same heavy crossbars and posts, ran plank catwalks eight feet high. They dropped.

"Damn," Cotton said. "I didn't think we'd run into anything like this. One of us should've come down here yesterday and had a look."

"How'd we know we'd be back?" they demanded.

"Well, we have to see where the gates are and how to do it. Somebody's gotta go out on that catwalk."

They panicked.

"Not me!"

"What if you fell off?"

"They'd mash you!"

"I can't stand high places!"

Cotton sighed. "What a hairy outfit. So I s'pose I have to."

"No," Goodenow said. "You've done enough. So's Teft. It isn't fair."

Shecker had one of his unfunny ideas. "Maybe you go in like in a bullring." He held a make-believe cape, he stamped a matador's foot. "Toro! Hah, toro! Then when they charge, open the gate—"

"Gas 'im," they snapped.

"Hey, I know," said Lally 1. "Draw straws. The shortest one walks the plank. I'll get some hay from those bales."

He was gone and back with a fistful and sorting lengths before they could think the method through.

"Cotton holds 'em," Teft said. "You cheat."

"I do not!"

"I get dizzy even on a chair," Goodenow pleaded.

"If it was only lighter," Cotton said. "Say, where's Lally 2?"

They chased their tails. The little stinker was always sneaking off, down a road or under a bed.

"No!" Cotton snapped his fingers. One leap and he stood on the third crossbar. The rest followed, the straws forgotten.

And there was Lally 2, already too far out to haul back, inching on hands and knees along the catwalk toward the center of the pens. It was so crucial to him that he had even left his pillow behind. *Box Canyon Boys Camp rented its horses reasonably from a resort near Phoenix which stabled them for dude guests in winter and needed a place to summer them out of the heat. For the most part they were indolent animals which required a hard leathering to get beyond a trot. Lally 2 was terrified of the one assigned to him, an elderly mare named Sheba. He refused to mount her, much less to ride. One night early in the session Cotton missed him, and scouting, found him seated on the corral fence talking to Sheba. "Are you a mother horse?" asked Lally 2. "Have you had some babies?" He hopped down, walked to the mare, and putting an arm over her neck, spoke into her ear. "Sheba, want to know where I sleep sometimes at home? In the sauna. There's some little people living there under the hot rocks. Ooms, that's their name, and hundreds of them come out and sleep with me." She whuffed and nuzzled his pajamas. "If you had any babies," he asked her, "did you stay with them or go galloping away and leave them?" Cotton brought a bridle from the barn, helped the boy mount, and led them around the corral. The next day Lally 2 rode her. After that he was aboard the mare most of the time. He could whisper in the ear of that old crowbait and make her perform like a show horse. They won the barrel race in the camp rodeo.*

Cotton was climbing, using a post for leverage, and hoisting himself. The rest were climbing, too, which he rather expected of them. Set them an example and they came through every time. Lally 2 was not all that intrepid, though. He waited for them.

The catwalk was made of two 2-by-6's nailed side by side and braced atop the inner wall which bisected the rectangle. In the dark the planking seemed about as wide as a snake's hips and as high as the Empire State Building. Along they crawled as though on combat patrol, noses to rumps—Kenilworth and Rocky River and Mamaroneck and Sixty-Fourth Street and Shaker Heights and Kenilworth. The system of pens began to make sense. They were holding pens, four large sections designed to hold the entire herd during roundups, to break it down into manageable bunches, and to cut individuals out for vaccination. Singly they could be driven into a small diamond-shaped squeeze pen in the center of the four-sectioned rectangle, and from it into the squeeze chute, a box of steel bars which trapped them and vised them immobile while the veterinarians gave them the needle. Fortunately, and necessarily, all the inner barriers including the gates in each were topped with catwalks, since no one in his right mind would enter a pen at ground level.

Just as the Bedwetters reached the center, the squeeze pen, the scud of clouds opened, and Lally 2, the leader, stopped. But the five behind him could not see, and cautiously, unsteadily, they stood up, and teetering, clasping hands, edged sideways on the planks. Then Lally 2 said "Oh!" And there they were, in their magnificence.

The buffalo is the largest, most awesome game animal found on the American continent. Standing six feet at the shoulders, even higher at the hump, measuring more than nine feet in length, the bulls weighed 2,000 to 2,600 pounds, the cows but a few hundred less. They tapered from mighty forequarters and heads and humps to slender hindquarters supported on delicate ankles and hooves, and beards of hair tufted from below their snouts and from their heads and legs and tails. Even in wan moonlight the curved, carved horns glinted, sleek hides tautened over muscle, eyes struck sparks of fire. And they were loco. Given reasonable situations, a man might reasonably guess how a buffalo would behave, but these beasts, deprived of the open range and comparative freedom they had

113

known from birth, cut out from the big herd and stockaded for three days without food and water and goaded by alien sounds and smells, were totally unpredictable.

What they did now, for example, by instinct, they had never done before. In the old days, one of the most remarkable sights on the prairies each spring was the thousands of circles where the grass had been trodden bare. "Fairy rings," the pioneers called them, unaware what had made them. In reality, they were formed by bull buffalo walking circular guard round and round the cows and calves to fend off wolf packs. And now, as the animals snuffed the odor of man nearby, of man their mortal enemy now, as they drew into flaring nostrils that scent which for the first time connoted death, half the herd advanced, the bulls, and stood on guard before the cows, snorting and stamping hooves, heads lowered to hook with horns whatever might attack.

Nothing would. Instead, high on the catwalk, holding on to each other, six boys quaked before the beasts below. They turned, they deflated, they crawled back as fast as they could along the planks to the squeeze pen. There, letting legs down, they sat like bumps on a log as what they had seen sank in. The enormity of the task hunched their shoulders. To liberate the herd they must get it through two pens: the squeeze and one of the big ones. Three gates had to be opened: one between the section in which the herd was now held and the squeeze pen; a second between the squeeze pen and a large; and a third in the outer wall of the large, which opened onto the range. And through those gates they must hoo-hah or sweettalk thirty tons of critters as mean as sin and twice as jumpy as they were themselves.

Cotton found some dried blood on his nose and peeled it off, thinking. Then he said it wasn't as tough as it looked. Here was how. The second and third gates they could open safely now, no sweat. He'd stay here on the squeeze pen by gate one. The rest of them would go back outside the way they came, around the corner to the section where the herd was. That would turn the buff toward them and away from him. Then he'd jump down, open number one gate into the squeeze pen, climb up again, and when they saw he'd done that here, all five of them should climb the pen wall above the herd, suddenly, together, and lean over and not holler but wave headgear and kick the crossbars and that ought to stampede the herd out past him and out the last two gates.

"Okay," he said. "Got it?" He knew they were petrified. "Okay," he said decisively, "Teft, you open two and three gates on your way. And for God's sake, when all of you get over there, when I jump down to open this one, give me time to get up again before you guys go up the wall. And remember, this is what we're here to do. Okay, everybody move on out."

Nobody budged. He despaired. And then, of all

unlikelies, Lally 1, on the end and more afraid his little brother would steal the show again than he was of the buffalo, took off on hands and knees and the rest followed.

Cotton watched them go. With this bunch, you never knew who or why or what next. They were as bad as buffalo. He watched Teft drop, open number two gate on the opposite side of the squeeze pen, climb to the catwalk again, crawl to the outer wall and open gate three. Then they disappeared into the night.

He tried to time them around the corner and along the wall. They'd be slow, he was sure of that, knocking knees and dragging tails. Then movement in the herd clued him. He stood up, sensing rather than seeing. It seemed to him the animals had wheeled, facing the wall away from him. He heard them snuff and stomp. Clouds had closed down and he could not tell, but they must be there now, revving themselves up to assault the wall, the herd acted like it. He pulled his helmet chinstrap tight. He crouched to jump. He tried to whisper Geronimo but his mouth was dry.

He jumped. The gate was secured with a chain and drop-bolt. The instant his bootheels hit dirt he reached for the chain and jerked the bolt and grabbing a crossbar swung the gate wide and in the same frantic sequence of movement leaped for the opposite wall and flew upward hand over hand and toe over toe before he got a horn up his rear.

Things happened so fast that Cotton nearly fell

off the catwalk. On the wall over the herd he thought he saw the flap of hats. Then he heard milling and that awful rumble and the hats vanished and there was a crash and splinter of wood and he thought, oh God they've smashed right through the pen wall. Then below him a bull and two cows tried to batter through the gate he'd opened and the whole squeeze pen swayed and he did fall, flat, flinging arms around the planks as the damnfool animals rushed through gate two into the big pen and instead of taking the last gate and cutting the scene wheeled and rammed right back through his gate and back into the original pen with the rest of the herd.

If Cotton could have, he'd have cursed loud enough to wake George Armstrong Custer. If he'd had cry time, he'd have flooded the pens with frustration and salt water. Instead, he jumped down, damn the danger now, shut gate two, and legged it out gate three and past the pickup and baled hay and panting, around the corner and along the outer wall, thinking, oh no, oh God, the buffalo went through that wall like a knife through butter with the guys on top of it and I did it, I got them slaughtered, because they're dead, every one of them dead!

14

HE COLLIDED WITH THEM IN THE DARK BY THE
lane. There were no casualties.

But they had come completely unglued again.
Lined against the fence, they embraced the wires
like long-lost friends and, stammering, managed to
tell him that a whole horde of bulls had charged the
wall while they were on it and almost torn it down,
and weak with relief, Cotton leaned against a
fencepost and removed his helmet and swabbed his
forehead with a sleeve.

"Where's my pillow?" lamented Lally 2.

"My feet are blistered," Goodenow complained.

"I knew we should've gone home," said Lally 1.
"We'd be in Flag by now except for my smartass
brother."

"Be kind to dumb animals bleah," Shecker said.

"Zap! Pow!" Teft marveled. "They hit that wall like the Green Bay Packers! Bam!"

"Can it," Cotton ordered wearily. "I gotta think." He listened. In the pen the buffalo were still milling, but at least the commotion had not roused the Arizona sportsmen from their tents and campers. And he listened to the Bedwetters whimper about no radios and how pooped they were and how cuckoo to attempt this in the first place. They were about to flake out on him again, he knew the signs. If it wasn't one nitpick crisis they overreacted to, it was another—a bird out of a tree, a police car startling them, running out of gas, and now being tossed off a wall by a few emotionally disturbed animals. And if they were nice, normal, cereal-eating, deodorant-using American kids he could slap them into shape—but they weren't. They were always up on a wall waving crazy hats. And crazy beasts were always charging them. He had to come up with a plan pronto. But first they needed the old vitamins and minerals.

"We better bump," he said. "C'mon."

They were doubtful.

"C'mon," he urged. He put his back to the fencepost, held hands out, and slowly, dubiously, they came to him and made the magic ring, then closed it tight, heads bowed.

They closed eyes.

Bracing and embracing each other, they bumped cheeks and noses gently, touching faces.

A minute passed, and two. Deaf, dumb, sightless,

but joined in hope and fear and the warm fur of their humanity, they stood guard over what they had created together that summer.

It worked again. The wolves were kept at bay.

Cotton opened his eyes. "Okay, men, hear this," he said. "We try it one more time."

Separating, they groaned for effect.

"We might as well, it's damn near morning and we're gonna be caught anyway with no wheels. We came close that time, believe it or not. After I open the squeeze gate, three of them did go through— but they're as shook up as we are and they came right back. So what we've gotta do is, without making noise, some way stampede 'em, the whole bunch, so they'll light out and keep going, and I know how."

What they'd do, he explained, was station two guys, one at the near squeeze gate he'd opened and one at the far. Gate three, to the range, would be left open. Then when the herd was through one and two, the two guys would jump down and close 'em to make sure none of the buff turned around. Burning rubber and with no place to go but out the last gate, they damn well would.

"Who'll be the two?" Goodenow interrupted.

"Me and Teft."

"No. That's not fair either." Goodenow was being ethical again. "Shecker and I will. We haven't done anything. I urped and he made us stop in Flagstaff to eat, so it's our turn to contribute."

With both hands, Shecker wrenched at the dagger in his chest. "Stabbed! Give me a break!"

Cotton clapped on his helmet. "Have it your way. But here's how we panic 'em. The other four of us climb the wall again, together, like before, only this time we flash flashlights at 'em and throw radios and hats into 'em and they'll go, I swear to God they will."

"Radios?" they asked hollowly. "Throw radios?"

"What else?" Cotton's voice hardened. "All of us know we're not just doing this for the buff. This is the last chance to find out what we've really got. What this summer adds up to. So let's find out. Goodenow and Shecker, give us your radios and flashlights and hats and take off. When our lights come on, get set for the action. We'll stay here till we think you're up on the squeeze pen and ready. Okay, men, this is it. Good luck. To us and them."

Shecker and Goodenow surrendered flashlights and transistors and the Hopi headband and Arnold Palmer's golf cap and went thoughtfully off along the wall. Cotton had his three, Teft and the Lally brothers, arrange gear in pockets so that they could throw in this order: flashlights, radios, hats. When he gave the signal, he said, jump up the wall, about three bars up, hang on with one hand and bomb with the other. That would do it, he said again. That damn well better do it.

They waited. On the other side of the wall the animals snuffed and bristled and waited, too. Cotton timed by low clouds covering and uncovering a decrepit star.

Scorned, they scorned. Cast out, they bunched. Impulses to call home they sublimated. The use of surnames became habitual.

Although he was not a natural leader, the authority Cotton had seized by he-man hocus-pocus, with razor and dogtags and cigar and whiskey, he held on to with claws and clamped jaws. If a fight with an outsider seemed obligatory, he fought it, losing invariably to bigger boys but taking his bruises with redheaded stoicism. Within the cabin he was friend and counselor and drill sergeant, coaxing his platoon along paternally at one moment, kicking it with ridicule the next. Deviants and dings they might be, short in saddle and inept with a rifle and butterfingered before a ground ball, but by the end of the fourth week, the middle of the session, the Bedwetters had turned a kind of psychoneurotic corner. The midnight ride to a movie let air out of their tensions and nailed up their tailbones. Their second raid shocked the entire camp into recognition.

Cotton conceived it. They executed it perfectly. Late one night they opened the corral gate and slapped the string into the pines, then ran hallooing through the camp: "Horses out! Horses out!" Lights went on, campers and counselors cursed and dressed and fanned out to round up the animals before they reached California. Since it had happened once before, someone's carelessness in closing the corral gate, no one suspected. Sticking together in the dark, the Bedwetters doubled back to the deserted camp. One by one they bagged the five trophies from the unguarded cabins, the buffalo, mountain lion, bear, bobcat, and antelope heads, and toting them to open ground, lined them in a row. Teft put a weird cherry on the triumph. Telling them to wait a minute, he loped off to the rifle range, brought back a .22 and cartridges, and standing over the prizes, fired a round between the glass eyes of each head. They scattered quickly then, rejoining the roundup in the woods and staying with it till the job was done and the corral full.

Discovery brought the camp out of its cabins a second time. Apaches, Sioux, Comanches, Cheyenne, Navajo—the tribes were enraged. The Bedwetters had to be the ones. They couldn't raid their rear ends without cheating. There was hot talk of retribution, of bedding them down for the rest of the night under a latrine, for instance. They stunk anyway. They broke rules. But the Director faced the lynch mob down, and ordering the accused to the chow cabin, he interrogated them. They admitted nothing. They sat in uneasy silence, Cotton scowling, Shecker biting his nails, Teft smiling, Goodenow twisting, Lally 1 making fists, and Lally 2 sucking his thumb.

Finally the Director lost his temper and told them they were sick. They belonged in some sort of institution, he wasn't sure which sort, but it wasn't a camp for normal boys, healthy in mind and body.

He would send them packing except that they had only four weeks left and he didn't wish to burden their parents, who were doubtless happy to be rid of them and deserved a respite. Therefore they could stay, conditionally. One more sick trick like this and he'd have them on the next plane out of Phoenix.

It was the bullets between the eyes which stunned Box Canyon Boys Camp. That was an aberrant act, a calculated discharge of hostility. It implied, the senior counselors muttered among themselves, a condition close to paranoia. Despised as usual by the other campers, even hated now, the psychos in Cotton's cabin were bullied and tormented no more, however. You dared not say it, but you were a little afraid of them because you never knew what vindictive thing they might do next. They spooked you.

Raiding ceased. It was no longer a game. Its meaning had been altered.

A lock was placed on the rifle rack.

There were no more ritual presentations of the chamber pot at the powwows on Saturday nights. The Bedwetters carried their fetish everywhere with them, as though they were proud of it.

In the darkness, Cotton nudged Teft and Lally 1 and 2. "Time," he whispered. "Remember— flashlights then radios then hats—and no noise."

Lally 2 extricated his thumb from his mouth. "Cotton?"

"What."

"What'll we do if they, if they come at us again instead of the other way they're s'posed to?"

"They won't," Cotton said. "I promise. Now—really throw hard—pretend you're heaving big, bitchin' hand grenades—here we go now—hit it!"

Two jumps to the wall and one, two, three crossbars up and they were leaning over, Cotton on one end, Teft on the other, the Lally brothers between, over the herd, confrontation of past and future, leaning over for a terrifying second in the stench and desperation of the beasts before flashlights snapped on and six yellow brands sailed into the pen and five radios and a shower of beads and cloth and plastic slapped humps and clattered horns and black shapes reared and bulk smashed against the wooden walls of 4-by-8's and a roar of hooves went up like a locomotive highballing and the herd was on its way.

They dropped. Wildly the four sprinted along the wall, hearing wood crack and bolts screech as the herd larruped through the squeeze pen. They turned the corner into a sudden vacuum of silence. They slowed, gulping. Goodenow and Shecker met them, arms extended, pointing.

Spent and dirty, the six boys stood bareheaded. What they had done was more immense than they had ever imagined. They quivered. Their toes sang songs. Their hearts beat poetry. Through the tingling gates of their fingertips their souls were liberated. For out on the range, in the last of the moon, leaping and kicking up heels as though at play, the buffalo ran free.

15

<hr/>

It was the finest moment of their lives. They awed themselves.

"Ahem." Cotton cleared his throat.

They stirred.

"Ahem. In my jacket," he said, embarrassed. "I've been saving it all summer. For when we did something really strong."

He dug deep into his pocket and brought out an object wrapped in toilet paper. "I packed these in the cabin before we left." As they gathered round him, he unwound the paper. Inside were three small bottles of whiskey, the size served on airlines.

"Wow," they said. "Where'd you get those?"

"Bagged 'em. On the plane coming out, while Teft was tearing up the place. It was easy. The stewardesses were having hernias and left the cart right by me. I got four. One I drank that morning after we loused up the first raid, you saw me. But we each get half a bottle now. We deserve it."

He showed them how to break the seal by unscrewing the cap. "Here's to the Bedwetters," he said, "the best damn buffalo cowboys in the West." He tipped the bottle and while they watched, had the first snort.

Cotton shared with Lally 2, Goodenow with Shecker, and Teft with Lally 1. They made a sacrament of it, there in the dark beside the empty pens, the others waiting respectfully while each one drank and puffed out his cheeks and swallowed hard to keep from choking. Goodenow was the most tentative, and when he went into a coughing fit, they pounded him companionably on the back. *Very studious, prefers reading to other activities. Has few friends. Phobic reaction to school continues and has recently manifested self-destructive tendencies. Roots of problem in home situation, which is still unresolved."* Goodenow's stepfather tore up this year-end report by the school psychologist. *The bigdomes had shanked their drives, he told Gerald's mother, and now it was his turn to tee off. There was a camp in Arizona—a friend mentioned it at the country club the other day—where boys learned to ride and shoot and dry out behind the ears, and that was where Gerald-baby was going this summer. Gerald's mother wept. Arizona was too far away, Gerald wasn't outdoorsy, he'd be thrown from a horse and crippled. Crippled hell, his stepfather roared. She had to choose. First, between a husband and an infant who still piddled his bed. And second, between what she wanted her offspring to be. Maybe he was only an engineer, not a head shrinker, but he could damn well tell the difference between a left-handed and a right-handed monkeywrench. Between male and female. And one of these days she'd better make up her mind about her home-grown, breastfed darling: either beat him into jeans and boots or buy him a dress and cosmetics.*

From the top of the stairs, Gerald listened.

When they had emptied the three bottles, they stood about solemnly and expectantly, sneaking glances at each other. A whole ounce of whiskey was sure to have some combustive effect. Lally 1 produced a belch, but on an empty stomach it was amateur.

Shecker realized he had an audience. Rather than an impersonation or one of his father's routines, he commenced a slow shuffle, bending arms at the elbows, swinging them, shuffling in a circle. They asked what that was supposed to be.

"Buffalo dance. Read it in some book. When the buff were gone, the Injuns blew their minds. Tried to dance 'em back. Danced till they dropped." He humped his head down, moving it from side to side, grunting: "Big Chief Shecker—heap firewater —him do dance—bring back buff—to Times Square."

The rest hesitated. And then, since it seemed

incumbent upon them to freak out in some alcoholic manner, they fell into line behind him—Teft and Goodenow and the Lally brothers. Bending at the waist, heads down and swinging, forearms pumps, they shuffled in a wide circle, huffing and puffing a guttural chant: "Huh-huh-huh-huh, huh-huh-huh-huh." They were surprised. They liked to dance. They heard the ghosts of drums, thumping. Old legends they pounded out by boot. Old shame they washed away in sweat. Out of old and bitter herbs they made new medicine. In gene and pride and whiskey they were restored. They stomped, they leaped, they hooked derision with their horns, chanting softly: "Huh-huh-huh-huh, huh-huh-huh-huh."

They stopped. They missed Cotton. He was up the wall, scouting over the pens toward the ranchhouse and the assembly of vehicles. They climbed up beside him.

"Hey, Cotton."

"Paleface no dance. How come?"

"Look up there," he said.

They did.

"Hour, hour and a half, it'll be light and the shooters'll be awake and loading guns. Somebody's gonna come down here to check the meat." He twisted about on the crossbar. "Now look out there."

They twisted.

"Look at those buffalo. They haven't gotten the

hell away. They're grazing, standing around being big and fat. I thought they'd be gone by now, out of sight, but they're too tame."

"So?"

"Tell it as it is."

"White man speak with hung tongue."

Cotton jumped, and sitting down, put his back to the crossbars. They jumped and squatted close to him. Unzipping his jacket, he fished inside his T-shirt for the dogtags round his neck, and jingling them out, told them with his fingers like beads.

"You got a problem?" asked Lally 2.

"Yup."

"What about?"

"Because we haven't done it yet. We haven't done a damn thing yet." His eyes burned at them, his words were indistinct with passion. "All we did was turn 'em loose and in the morning they'll be rounded up again and slaughtered—those shooters came here for thirty animals tomorrow and they'll have 'em—so we drink booze and dance our asses off and go home and we haven't accomplished a goddam thing!"

Cotton's generation grew up with a war in the house. For them, games of cops and robbers and cowboys and Indians no longer satisfied the senses. A boy had but to turn a control to be totally involved in the violent distension of experience that was Vietnam on television. Cotton became addicted to it. Vietnam was even a portable war. A boy had but to move his personal set to have air strikes in the

*living room, search-and-destroy operations in the
bedroom, naval bombardment in the bathroom—
napalm before school, body bags before dinner.
Cotton carried a battle map in his brain. His
imagination bristled with an arsenal of advanced
weaponry. Dak To and Khe Sanh were more real to
him than Anzio or the Little Big Horn. His former
fantasies, being the first man on the moon or
connecting with a touchdown pass in the Super
Bowl, he put away as childish, preferring instead to
slog through a rice paddy with a decimated platoon,
to exhort it to victory, to have a leg lopped off and be
decorated in the White House. His only fear was
that Vietnam might be over before he could get
there.*

*They lived on the lake in Rocky River, a suburb of
Cleveland, his mother and he. One evening after the
news, switching channels between the networks to
catch the complete war coverage, he slogged into her
bedroom and lay in the prone firing position on her
bed as she prepared herself at her dressing table for a
party. She applied a makeup base, brushed and
mascaraed her eyes, then fastened on false lashes.
He remembered how, after only one day's fishing in
Quebec, she had demanded to be flown out to
civilization, she was bored. She lined her eyelids
with pencil, and penciled a dot at the inner corner of
each eye. Her tennis game was slipping, he had
noticed. She was no longer a tigress at the net. With
a brush and color from a silver paintbox she shad-
owed each lid. She indulged him one day, disci-*

plined him the next. On each cheekbone she dabbed cream rouge, then smoothed it in. It occurred to John how frightened she must be, of middle age and loneliness and social insecurity and, underneath, even of him, because he would soon be a man. She blended two tones of lipstick on her mouth, overlaying the blend with white and kissing Kleenex to blot. To remain a girl, he realized, she had to keep her son a boy. Putting perfume behind her ears she smiled at him in the mirror. "Isn't your mother simply fabulous?" she asked.

"What're you scared of?" he asked. "Getting old?"

"Don't be nasty."

"I'm not," he said. "I'm fifteen. Try gooping that over. In one year and ten months I'll be seventeen. You want to know what I'm gonna do on my seventeenth birthday?"

"I'm listening."

"Join the Marines. You can if your parent signs the papers."

"Which I won't of course."

"Which you will. You'll be on the booze to celebrate my birthday—you won't even know what you're signing. But if you won't, I'll make a big sign and walk up and down in front of the Cleveland Yacht Club. 'My mother's forty-two years old,' that's what'll be on it."

"I'd kill you," she said.

And then, glaring into the mirror, she went white under her makeup. Behind her, elbows propped on

the velvet bedspread, John Cotton sighted her in as
though over the barrel of an M-16.

They shivered. The air was colder now, and the
dance dried upon their skins. It was that last,
impotent hour between darkness and dawn, when
men buy truth and sell illusions.

Gentle them, Cotton warned himself, gentle
them. They've given about all they've got. More
than they even knew they had. They're really only
kids yet, and you pop your cork and they'll go
ki-yiing into those pens and start tearing hair and
eating fingernails and dreaming bad and never
come out. But they've almost got it made. Only two
more miles. So give it to them easy. A slice of
watermelon at a time.

"You know I'm leveling," he told them. "The
whole idea was to save those buffalo. And we have
almost. And almost is only a couple miles from
here. I talked to one of the Game and Fish guys
yesterday—it's only a couple miles from here to the
fence at the back of this preserve. Other side of the
fence is the Mogollon Rim. All we gotta do is take
'em there and drive 'em through. Then they're
really free."

Standing up, he stuffed his dogtags and zipped
his jacket as though they were going to town to take
in a chocolate soda. "Okay, let's move. We've got
maybe an hour before daylight, and the tough part's
over. This doesn't take hair, just smarts. And
think—they'll scatter over a hundred square miles.

They'll have the whole state of Arizona for a preserve."

But they stayed hunkered. "How do we get 'em out?" asked Lally 1.

"Simple. The same way Game and Fish brought 'em in. With a Judas truck. There's damn little grass on that range, the guy told me. All they did was feed 'em hay out of a Judas truck and they followed like a flock of sheep. They haven't been fed for three days, they're starving."

"Starving, who isn't?" said Shecker. "I don't get the picture yet."

"Oh, come on, let's appreciate ourselves!" Cotton grinned. "We're professionals, we can do anything—we've proved it!" He pointed. "There's the hay—we serve it on a silver platter!" He pointed. "There's the truck—the Bedwetters ride again!" He pointed. "And there's Teft!"

Up shot Teft, the aircraft saboteur. Tilting over them, he came to attention, clicked heels, whipped something from a pocket, and stiffarming a Nazi salute, held the hotwire high. *"Sieg Heil!"*

16

T HE NIGHT DARKENED. A CORTEGE OF LOW BLACK
clouds lagged over them and let down rain in veils.
But they had cat's eyes now and much to do and did
not care about the rain.

Lally 2 went into the pens to salvage any usuable
flashlights or radios or headgear.

Teft inspected the pickup.

Cotton, Shecker, Goodenow, and Lally 1 loaded
hay. The bales were heavy, a hundred to two
hundred pounds, and even after lowering the tailgate it took a boy on each corner to heave and slide
them into the bed.

Lally 2 returned with one transistor which might
work. Everything else was wrecked, he said, including the hats, unless somebody wanted to walk
around with a pile of buffalo crap on his head.

Teft reported the truck was a state Ford, only two or three years old, with good rubber and plenty of petrol to make two miles, he was sure this time because he could hear it slosh in the tank as they loaded. He was already wired in and ready to roll.

They toiled five bales into the bed, raised the tailgate, added the rifle and, at Goodenow's insistence, the head and horns trophy, and were mounting up when Cotton remembered.

"Hey, the pillow," he said.

"Leave it," said Lally 2.

"Leave it?" said his brother. "Hah."

"You sure?" Cotton asked.

"I'm sure," said Lally 2 with dignity. "And don't make a big thing out of it."

The sibling rivalry between Lally 1 and 2 bordered on the psychotic. Incapable of controlling his impulses, Lally 1 vented his hatred of his brother overtly on still another occasion after his slaughter of the pets. Lally 2 won the barrel race in the camp rodeo. A timed event, each rider spurred from a standing start fifty yards to an equilateral triangle of three upright oil drums, circled each as rapidly and cleanly as possible by leaning from the saddle and guiding with reins, then booted his mount back to the start. Shortest elapsed time took first, and such was the almost mare-and-foal relationship between Sheba and Lally 2 that they clocked a three-second margin over the second-place pair. It was the summer's only win in anything by any of the Bedwetters. Within minutes, someone noticed black smoke fun-

neling from their cabin. The camp took off on the run. Lally 1 had set fire to the foam-rubber pillow his brother had brought from home, the one he couldn't sleep without, the one with which he withdrew under beds. By the time it could be doused in a toilet, half of it had scorched and fumed away.

"Hold it," Cotton said. He was just over the tailgate. "How we gonna break this bailing wire?" He worked both hands under the wire banding a bale and pulled in vain. "Teft, see if there's a pair of pliers or something in the cab."

Teft said no.

"Damn," Cotton said.

"You weakling Wasps," said Shecker. "This takes a guy from the ghetto." Picking up the .22, he thrust the barrel under a strand and began to twist the weapon clockwise. Under his fat, he was very strong. Presently the wire snapped.

Goodenow would have cheered had Cotton not shushed him. "Cool it, or the shooters'll be down here triggering us. They don't give a damn what they kill, just so it's alive. Okay, everybody set? Teft, no headlights, remember, and when she starts—I mean if—don't gun 'er, take it real slow. Okay, turn 'er over."

They waited.

"Blast off, Teft," Cotton said.

They waited.

Then a long, apologetic arm was extruded from the cab window like plastic. From the fingers, something dangled.

Perfection was required of Lawrence Teft, III. It was expected, too, that he would attend Exeter and Dartmouth, his father's schools. Since his grammar school record was one of underachievement, his father took him to New Hampshire in March to petition the headmaster personally. Through sleet they strode across the quad to the Administration Building, known to students as the Kremlin. They met the headmaster, were seated, and in the midst of his father's peroration on the justice of shaving admission standards for sons of contributing alumni, Lawrence interrupted with a vivid account of his car theft career, adding that so far as he was concerned, Exeter could shove itself up its own anal orifice. In the respiratory silence which ensued, the headmaster asked the boy to step outside so that the two men might confer. Politely he did. There he found the bowl of apples provided for students by the Principal's Fund. He ate one and fired the remainder out a window. In his absence, the headmaster advised his father to send the boy to a military school or a summer camp far from home. What was needed, in his opinion, was discipline—that and the maturation which would one day enable him to compromise, and hence to adjust to the realities of his environment. He recommended a camp near Prescott, Arizona. That was why, in June, his family put Lawrence Teft, III, aboard the plane at Kennedy like a prisoner.

Keys dangled from his fingers. He stuck his head out the window, an asinine smile on his face. "The keys," he said. "I forgot to look first. They left the keys in. Imagine that."

"For God's sake," said Cotton.

"Here we go."

The engine started at once. But the transmission declaimed, the truck jumped and stuttered, and the five in back were nearly unhorsed.

"Teft, what in hell you doing!" Cotton barked.

Teft's head appeared. "Keep your seats, gents. I never bagged anything like this panzer before. It's got a four-speed shift on the column—I think—and a low and high two-wheel and four-wheel drive stick on the floor—I think—and I dunno what I'm in. There will be a brief intermission."

They waited again. On the second try, Teft got them away equably, easing the Ford around the hay bales and pointing it toward the open range.

Rain ceased. The air was washed. Under a sky void of stars the Judas truck crawled out upon the preserve. It was as though they were setting humble sail upon a crusty sea, for the table of land lifted beneath them in long and glacial billows, cresting into the unknown. There was good grass here in spring, after the snows, and in the autumn, when storms drove moisture deep, but this had been a dry summer and the range was wizened. In the bed of the pickup the five knelt on bales and peered ahead over the roof of the cab. They picked out shapes. The herd was still bunched, nosing for weeds. The truck crept nearer.

A hundred yards off, Teft stopped and periscoped

his head. "Pardon me for asking, but I've never associated with buffalo much. What's the plan?"

"Let's get our signals straight," Cotton said. "From here on, I'll tap on the window. One means stop, two means go. Okay?"

"Great. But I mean now, what do we do right now? What's the protocol?"

Cotton hesitated, and even a second's doubt was enough to open the anxiety box.

"What if they charge us?" Goodenow wondered. "What if—"

"Look what they did to that pen," worried Lally 1. "If they can crack lumber like that, they could tip this whole truck over and—"

"What you do is," Shecker began, "go up to 'em and shake hands and say 'Soul Brother' in their ear—"

"Gas 'im," they said.

Cotton dropped the lid. "Can the chatter. The Game and Fish guy said they're practically pets and very hot for hay. And if this is the truck they haul it in, they'll know it."

"They don't know us, though," said Lally 2.

"Well, we gotta try," Cotton said impatiently. "The main thing is, don't bug 'em. They have to trust us. So no jumping around or talking. So listen, Teft, take it really slow, in the lowest gear you got. Head right into 'em."

Teft's ears cocked like a mule's. "Right into 'em?"

"Like we do it every day. When we're in the middle, and I tap once, stop."

"Stop? In the middle?"

"Okay," Cotton said, "everybody back here sit down right where you want to be for a while. And stay down. And stay loose."

Slowly they settled themselves on hay bales.

"Okay, Teft," Cotton said.

"Holy cow," Teft said.

He engaged low gear and inched toward the herd. The animals stopped grazing. Heads swung. Then they turned, the bulls first, to see and smell and classify. Perhaps they disbelieved what they saw.

Through the darkness toward them crept a monster. On its back it carried its young, a freight of whitefaced whippersnappers. One gripped a stick of steel and wood. Another held by a horn the noble bust of a king of their own kind.

For their part, the closer they came the less the Bedwetters believed what they were doing— entering a herd of monsters whose mood and power no man could assess. Of their own free, foolish will they were laying life and limb on the line.

Hood and bumper of the Judas truck intruded. The animals made way. The herd parted. In the middle, Teft heard a tap on the window at his back. He braked, and shoved the gearshift into neutral.

There was no sound except the panting of the exhaust, the random click of hoof on pebble. The buffalo drew near. Then buffalo surrounded the truck, bulls and cows, fierce horns and shaggy beards and great humps near enough to touch. Cotton, Shecker, Goodenow, Lally 1 and 2 sat on their bales like rigid digits. No one dared bat an eye or scratch an itch. They were truly frightened.

Beasts and boys considered each other. They smelled each other. And suddenly boys of fifteen, fourteen, and twelve were children once more. The breath of innocent animals blessed them. An emotion filled them, a tenderness that none of them had ever known. Peace descended on them, and they were not afraid. For a moment, or moments, it was as it had been in the beginning, before fear, before evil, before death, at the time of the creation, when the earth was new and living things flourished therein, when the earth was fair and all living things dwelt together as kindred. For a moment, or moments, beasts and children were friends, there in the sweetness and silence of the night, there in the calm and lovely fields of the Lord.

"Hello, buffalo."

Lally 2, the youngest, spoke to the beasts as he had spoken to his horse. To the thin pipe of his voice they listened patiently.

"Hello," he said. "Are you hungry? We're going to let you out. Then you can go anywhere and do anything. Just like you used to. We've got lots of hay in here. So come with us and eat. Come with us and nobody'll ever shoot you or hurt you again. Because we're going to let you go."

He pulled a fistful of hay from the unbound bale

and dropped it over the side of the pickup. The nearest animal, a cow, lowered her head and began to eat.

The other boys did likewise. Tearing clumps of fodder they tossed them into the herd, and huge heads went down at once for food.

Cotton tapped twice on the glass behind him. The truck moved.

143

17

And the herd followed, plodding along alert for the next offering of hay. It was exactly as the state employee had told Cotton. These were practically barnyard buffalo, hell on the hoof if riled but born on the preserve and accustomed throughout their lives, when the natural pickings were slim, to being fed from a truck like cattle.

Cotton called down to Teft to keep an eye peeled for the fence.

Using the rifle, Shecker the strongman snapped the wire on all the bales. Then the boys made themselves comfortable, lolling on the bales with backs against the cab, pulling wisps and streamers and dropping them over the sides or sailing them into the air to keep the herd on the go. They pulled off boots, they ventilated feet, they wigwagged ecstatic toes.

"The BC," Goodenow said. Then he giggled. "The Before Christ!" And that gave them the yips. They were ravenous for laughter. They hugged each other, they rolled off the bales, they combed each other's hair with hay. Whether it was the spectacle of thirty Disney animals following them or the residual effects of airline whiskey or the transformation of ripsnort penbenders into contented cudchewers or because it was the first time in hours they could cut loose above a whisper, they had hysterics.

Sid Shecker made $40,000 a week playing Las Vegas. Nightly, after the second show, he stopped in the casino to shoot dice and lose large sums and panic Sammy's mother. "So I lose five thousand, I make a hundred times that a year, I should keep my health," Sid would defend himself. "When you got money in this country," he would say to her and the children, "to the goyim you're somebody. So you should remember. Money we got, somebody we are." Sammy's mother, however, was inconsolable. Sometimes she waked the boy at two in the morning and dressed him and sent him downstairs, where he stood in the hotel lobby near the crap tables, a tousled, drowsy reminder, in case his father should see him, of Sid Shecker's indebtedness to family and mortality.

One night, after Sammy had waited an hour, Sid

145

swept him along to the coffee shop in his train of agents, managers, admirers, and moochers. The famous comic was in a savage mood. He had just lost six G's, and although his retinue did its greasy best to divert him, Sid was inconsolable. Noting that his son was devouring a piece of chocolate pie, Sid Shecker offered a wager: fat his Sammy might be at twelve already, but he would bet a thousand dollars the boy could inhale a dozen pieces of pie in four minutes, or twenty seconds each, not counting the one before him. Those at the table quickly covered the bet. Two chocolate pies were brought and cut. Watches were synchronized, time called, and Sammy dug in, determined to please his father. During the third piece he began to cry. His fingernails needed biting, he wanted to beg for lemon or cherry or coconut, but there was no opportunity between swallows. His belly churned with woe, his cheeks and chin were martyred with chocolate and whipped cream and tears. At the first bite into the eleventh piece Sammy yielded his fork. As the crowd at the table averted its face, Sid Shecker marched him to the elevator. There, on the way up to their suite, father gave son a piece of paternal advice: always play it big. So you gambled. Gamble big. So you were a fresser, a pig. Be a big fresser.

The Bedwetters laughed more than they needed to. Hilarity they perverted into a mechanism of defense, a step backward from the brink of nervous exhaustion on which they teetered. But it betrayed them. It pushed them over. And when they hit bottom they bounced up with the wibbles and came down with the eeks. Their ears turned into ashtrays, their crotches puckered into coin purses, and though they straddled the bales again and resumed tending the herd, they operated out of a trance. Even their conversation was unstructured. Snatches of memory, handfuls of anecdote were dropped over the sides of the pickup or tossed into the night of no moon. Only now and then were they coherent, even to each other.

"What day's it?" someone asked.

It had been years since they galloped out of Box Canyon Boys Camp.

"That book I read," said Shecker. "About the big dance. Also it said they used to stop trains and everybody got out and shot buffalo for the fun of it."

"What were you jokers laughing about?" Teft asked.

They shrugged. He had writhed himself through the cab window and seated himself on the sill, head and body outside, long legs inside. He steered with a bootheel.

"How can you drive that way?" someone asked him.

"Perfectly."

"Nineteenth of August," someone guessed. "The day it is."

They could scarcely recall stealing the first pickup in Prescott.

Cotton grubbed in his jacket pocket, struck a

match, lit another cigar, his second of the summer, and held the match to his wrist. "Geez, it's five-ten. Last time I looked it was three o'clock. We've dinked away two whole hours. Any minute now it's daylight and we're in trouble."

"Relax," someone said.

"Relax! I will when they're through that fence and not before!"

"I mean, what day of the week is it?"

The incident with the gunslingers and their hotrod in Flagstaff was fantasy.

Cotton drew on his cigar. "You guys see why letting 'em out of the pens wasn't enough. When they're out this time, they're really out. After tonight there'll be thirty buff loose in this state. You might see one anytime. A real live buffalo, like in the old days. We're doing something for the West. Which has done one hell of a lot for us."

"Wednesday?"

"I think."

"Saturday we go home."

"Home," they said. The word was meaningless.

"Besides," Teft said. "I was feeling alienated in the cab. From society. What was so funny?"

"I can see some old fud from Joisey driving along," said Shecker. "Look, Myrtle, a buffalo! And she flips."

"My stepfather told my mother, I heard him," said Goodenow. "To make up her mind if I was a boy or a girl."

"I wonder how our horses are," said Lally 2. "I hope asleep."

"Or some real hippies from California," said Lally 1. "On their way East tripped out on speed or something and they see a buffalo. Hey, man, where we at? What we on?"

"Little kids, too, seeing one," said Lally 2. "It'll be better for them than TV."

The truck growled along in some low gear, the herd in its wake, heads bobbing as though in line in some crazy cafeteria. Cotton was up every couple of minutes, searching over the cab into the dark reaches. The fence obsessed him, and the imminence of morning. They must have covered two miles by now, he insisted, they had to have.

"Two mph," said Teft, "is not exactly burning up the track. No sweat. She can't stall and you can't even cut the ignition, because she's wired twice. Mine and Hank Ford's."

"Cotton was right," said Goodenow. "To make us finish no matter what. It's good for our characters."

"It's like Ralph," Teft agreed.

"Who?" someone asked.

"Ralph. My cousin's piranha."

18

WHAT'S A PIRANHA?" ASKED LALLY 2.

"A fish. Only it eats meat."

"Don't mention food," said Shecker.

"I've got this cousin goes to Amherst," Teft explained. "He bought this baby piranha and named it Ralph and took it to school and kept it in an aquarium in his room and every day fed it a fresh goldfish from the dimestore. Goldfish really turn a piranha on."

"Go easy on that hay," Cotton warned.

"There's some little people who live in our sauna," said Lally 2, "under the rocks. They make the steam."

"So Ralph got bigger and bigger and needed more goldfish and my cousin was running back and forth to the dimestore buying goldfish and destroying his academic life. He loved Ralph but this spring he knew they had to part. So he put him in a pail and drove him over to some girls' college around there where they have a goldfish pond and dumped him in. The pond was loaded with these big, gross goldfish."

Goodenow propped the trophy between his legs, holding it upright by the horns. He gazed into the red, ferocious eyes under Teft's bullethole.

"I said go easy on the hay," Cotton said. "In case you haven't noticed, we're down to under two bales. Start rationing them."

"Well, when Ralph got into that pond with those gross goldfish, he went berserk. He turned gourmet. All he ate out of them was their fat bellies. One bite, gulp, one belly, and every morning there'd be dead goldfish floating around with their bellies missing. Which was where old Ralph made his mistake."

"What mistake?" someone asked.

"Tell me," Goodenow said to the trophy. "Did you live up here? Were you Superbull? Do you appreciate what we're doing for your friends and relatives?"

"Because the gardeners at the girls' college knew something was fishy. They took the rest of the goldfish out and poisoned the pond and old Ralph went to his reward. Because he made a piranha pig of himself."

They pondered. To analyze anything made their skulls ache, and the irrelevance of the story irked them. "Teft," they snarled.

"Yup."

"What's the point?"

"Point?"

"I haven't seen the Chicago Cubs play all summer," said Lally 2. "I've been culturally deprived."

"The message!" they bawled. Teft frequently let them hang by their fingernails. "What's the message!"

"Oh," said Teft. "Well, if old Ralph had devoured whole goldfish instead of being picky, the gardeners might not have caught on for a long time. Ralph might be alive and well and living in that pond right now. But he didn't. So the moral is, don't just eat bellies."

"Bellies!"

"I wish I had a whole chocolate pie," said Shecker.

"Eat everything," said Teft.

"Eat everything!"

"I mean, finish what you start." Teft shook his head, amazed at their density. "You know, like at the Grand Canyon, remember?"

"My timmy brother and me," said Lally 1, "did we have a ball on a boat once." *The psychiatrist in Lucerne was world-renowned for his work with children. Stephen and Billy Lally went to see him from the villa their mother had rented for the summer. They expected the Swiss would be some old turkey with a beard and ask stupid questions. He was young and clean-shaven. He took Stephen into a room filled with toy human figures made of plastic.*

Selecting four, a man, a woman, and two boys, and opening cabinets of costumes, he asked Stephen to dress the four dolls, which were to represent the members of his family, in costumes appropriate to the role played by each in his, Stephen's, opinion. Stephen Lally, Jr., dressed the two boy-dolls in men's suits and the two adult dolls in little-boy and little-girl clothing. The psychiatrist said that was very interesting and they would talk about what it meant the next time. But there was no next time because their father flew over to Europe and made up with their mother and they all sailed home together on the United States, *a very fast ship. The two brothers had fun one night during the crossing. Sneaking up to the Sun Deck, they let all the passengers' poodles out of their kennels. Soon there were poodles everywhere aboard ship, racing through the theater, barking in the bars.*

Attending even partially to Teft's dumb story, they had neglected to feed, and now the buffalo closed in around the truck. Humps and beards and hot breath and hallucinations menaced them on three sides. Trapped, they squidged close to each other on the iron floor of the bed. Oddball ideas bumbled through the alleys of their heads. Who, it occurred to them to wonder, was herding who? Which were the shepherds now, and which the sheep?

"Dammit, we're losing our marbles!" Cotton cried. "Teft, you're going in circles or we'd be there!"

Teft was insulted. "Okay, U-Drive-It."

"You know I can't!" Cotton jabbed with his cigar. "Get back in that cab and turn on the lights once and see if you can see that fence!"

Teft grudged through the window and Cotton barked at the others. "Give 'em hay before they come in here and take it! But not too much!"

They were down to a bale and a pile. Under Cotton's supervision they commenced to pay the hay out in wisps. Teft tried the headlights once but no luck, no fence. Cotton was up and down again, drawing on his cigar, perturbed about goofing off on the hay as they had on gas.

"But there's more of 'em now," argued Lally 1. "There's a lot more'n thirty out there."

They strained eyes, counting. Shecker made out forty-one animals, Goodenow forty-two.

"New customers," said Cotton. "Great. The more join up, the more make it."

"Hey, and look!" squealed Lally 2. "Little ones!"

Beyond the cluster of bulls and cows, two buffalo calves skipped on stick legs beside their mothers. Born in May or June, they had no horns as yet, nor humps, and their lambs' tails twitched at the pleasure of reunion with their aunts and uncles.

"Forty-one and two calves," Shecker said. Then he clapped his forehead. "We're counting! We can see!"

"Morning!" they cried. "Wow! We've been up all night!"

They were on their feet in a flash, steadying each other, gaping at the strangers with whom they had shared the long dark hours and danger and fulfillment, at the measles of mud and blood on their faces, at the stubble of hay in their hair. They were a sorry corps of desert canaries, and too tired to chirp.

Turning from each other, they looked about them. Day had not come. But night was surely gone. They traveled by no map toward no horizon. The world was made of milk. Land and sky were one skimmed gray. And they were in some pinch-me place. It might have been Arizona or Africa or Asia or the barebutt of the moon. But the buffalo were real. Black within the gray, not brown, and mightier than they had been in the pens, they whuffed and bumped and masticated and walked in one black, primordial exodus. And the truck was real, too. The exhaust throated. Spit out from under tires, stones pinged. Guitars thrummed. Drums boomed a big beat. A singer implored.

"The radio!" they whooped.

They seized Lally 2 and practically ripped off his jacket getting out the transistor. It worked! Some sweetheart of a station had come on the air, some dear, sleep-drunk DJ had spun the first beloved platter!

"James Brown!"

"His Famous Flames!"

"Let's hear it for the Japs!"

"Hooooooooray!"

They turned up the volume. The big beat revived them. Shuffling on stocking feet about the bed and through the hay they snapped fingers and flipped hips.

"Yeah, yeah!"

"Sock it to me!"

"Bitchin'!"

Shecker raised the transistor over his head and waved it at the herd, saying this was how the nightriders used to lullaby the longhorns on the trail to Dodge City in the good old days, with Jap radios and James Brown and His Famous Flames.

"Shut up! Everybody shut the hell up!" Cotton hammered with a fist on the cab roof, deafening Teft. "And turn that damn thing off!" he railed. "And get down in here and feed! Whatta you got—beans for brains? Don't you know back there they've already found their truck and herd gone and any minute now that whole sportsman army'll be after us to kick our ass from here to Mexico? Or try us for target practice? They let go with a thirty-thirty and you'll dance, by God, you'll dance till you're on your knees!"

They settled down immediately. Lally 2 returned the radio to his jacket. They fed again, gleaning from the floor and beginning on the last bale. Cotton turned his back on them, concentrating over the cab, cigar sputtering like a fuse. Once he glanced at his wrist. It was five thirty-four. Twice he ate Teft out for not being capable of driving a straight line for two miles and locating a simple damn fence. Behind him, the rest resigned themselves. His outburst might have provoked a response had they not recognized the familiar symptoms: he was charging his aggressive batteries again, readying himself for the downhill road to one of his uptights.

The dawn was lavender now. They drifted on a raft through vast and lavender waters. A kelp of creatures followed in their wake, tossing horns impatiently at the scant fare offered them. There were more mouths to feed than ever, for six fullgrown specimens had joined the school, flippering in on lavender tides.

"Cotton?"

What he'd said about being on their knees was troubling them, but only Lally 2 dared address him now.

"Cotton, will we have to go to jail?"

He faced them. "Prob'ly. For bagging two pickups at least. And blowing a hole in a tire. And being juvenile delinquents, fugitives from camp and our folks. There's enough, that's for sure." He tapped ash over the side. "But if we get 'em out, it'll be worth it. If we don't, if we foul up when we're this close—"

"I mean, what'll they do to us?" asked Lally 2. "The hunters."

"Who knows? But they're not hunters, they're

meatmen. And anybody who'll shoot animals to pieces for kicks the way they did yesterday'll do anything."

"Maybe they'll put us in the pens instead," said Lally 1.

"And let us out three at a time," said Shecker.

"And chase us with horses till we can't run any more," gloomed Goodenow.

"Cotton!" Teft's head was out the window. "Hey, you guys—the fence!"

Sliding on socks, falling over each other, the Bedwetters jumped to the lookout over the cab.

"Oh, no," Cotton groaned. "Oh, no."

19

None of them had thought about the fence which must bound the preserve on its south side. They had assumed it would be the four-strand bobwire which enclosed the pens and ranchhouse area. Now they knew better. There, several lines of ordinary wire and sets of cattleguards sufficed to keep the buffalo out of the streets and bars of Flagstaff. But here, where the temptation to go gallivanting off into a paradise of pine and canyon would be considerable, the single restraint must be as sure as scripture. It was.

Teft had stopped the truck. To galvanize them, Cotton barked boots on, everybody, but the troops had difficulty even matching boots to feet. Then, to hold the herd where it was, he had them scatter half of the remaining bale.

Color changed. The world blushed. Pink and

159

psychedelic boys served pink and psychedelic beasts.

That done, he had Teft gun away from the herd and pull alongside the fence. It was chainlink iron, eight feet high and strung taut between iron posts deepset every ten yards. Pieces of shag hung from it where the animals had rubbed to rid themselves of their winter robes. From the truck bed they could see over—a pink sky and a few pines and beyond, the Mogollon Rim.

"Let's not stand around like turkeys—push!" Cotton put his shoulder to the fence. "C'mon, lay on it!"

The other three put theirs, but after the first dubious effort, they merely leaned. Seven hours of hyperactivity and a sacrifice of radios and headgear and a final, spastic dance had drained them. Trembling, mouths dry, they called it quits and slumped to the floor too whipped to care what Cotton might say. O twayne me a twim, where the ffubalo jym.

A raw red sun of August chinned itself on the horizon. A new day dazzled.

Cotton said nothing. Both arms extended, fingers, claws around the links, legs as bowed as staves, head down, dead cigar vised in his jaws, he fought it out with the fence alone. What the taxes of iron and stress and night and day and life and death and flesh and wish exacted, he would not pay. What a bull buffalo could not do, he must.

But this time he was not granted surcease. This time he was incapable of compromise. Twisting his body about, he put his back to the fence and braced his boots. The tendons in his neck corded just as light flared over his face and his eyes flew open and the cigar dropped from his mouth and he stared, transfixed, then pointed over their heads.

"Here they come!"

That reared them staring, too, behind them, out over the preserve. The light of the rising sun had been refracted from the windshield of a jeep a mile away as though by heliostat. The jeep was followed closely by two pickups, both filled with human figures. Boiling dust behind them, the three vehicles topped a rise and dropped out of sight into a trough.

"Too late, damn us, we're too late!" Cotton sobbed, as though the Bedwetters were to blame for the morning, then yelled: "No, we're not—Teft! Back to the herd—slow—don't spook 'em—go, go!"

As the truck returned he pushed the others to their knees. Unbolting the tailgate, he kicked it down with a clang and the second Teft stopped, had them sweep the floor of the bed clean of the half-bale and litter.

"That'll hold 'em! Now take us away, Teft! Fifty yards—over there—but slow! Go, go!"

He was desperate and sane and improvising and coordinated and stoical as stone and chiggers of excitement ate him alive. The Ford still rolling, he vaulted over the end with the rifle and ordered everybody out, Teft included, and move easy, buffalo would charge a man on foot without reason or warning. But they could no longer move under their own power. Tripped out on adventure and sleeplessness and hunger, they had wibbled away to Disland without saying good-by. They were disoriented, dissociated, discombobulated. He had to pull them and push them and place them a safe distance from the feeding herd. They stood like zombies, splaylegged and deaf and dumb to the proximity of dangerous animals and dangerous men. It was as though they were spectators at a happening which Cotton was creating for their pleasure. O twayne me a twim, where the ffubalo jym, where the rede and the telopen zoom.

Cotton told Teft to load the rifle and the next time the lead jeep appeared over a rise, to fire. "Don't hit anybody, aim for the radiator," he said calmly. "Just scare 'em, make 'em stop."

Teft mumbled he couldn't, he couldn't hit the broad side of a barn.

"None of us can. Here." He made Shecker sit down and Teft sit behind him and use his shoulder as a rest. "Now you can. Now load."

Goodenow and the Lally brothers watched the game. Teft fumbled a round into the chamber and pushed the bolt home. The vehicles reappeared, nearer and coming fast over the range, in line and loaded with men.

"Fire," Cotton said.

"Cotton, I can't."

"Fire, goddammit!"

The .22 cracked. At that altitude they could hear the round hiss. The herd lifted heads, listening, but stayed put.

"Now keep on firing!" Cotton yelled. "Fire till you hit something and they stop! They'll be here in two minutes and I need three!"

Teft reloaded and fired again. Shecker cringed and the jeep stopped, the pickups behind it, the men in big hats piled out.

"Teft, you gotta get me three minutes!"

Teft looked around, but Cotton was gone.

Tangled, they were sent into simplicity. Unloved, they were committed to an institution of wind and space and tree sounds and the tonic smells of animals. It was a dispassionate place, the West. Mountains made no demands of them. The sky, wider than any they had ever known, was impartial. They underwent a therapy of sun and cliff and asylum, they were redeemed by a balm of days indistinguishable one from another. And they were healed, or seemed to be. While the Bedwetters might not yet do the merely difficult, they were finding on the hidden staircases of their personalities a compulsion to attempt the improbable—a talent, even, for the spectacular. A movie forbidden them they broke out to see at risk of expulsion. Tokens they could not win in competition they seized by guile, then desecrated with bullets. These exploits annealed them. The climax, the feat which liberated them at last, however, was the Grand Canyon hike. Cotton pulled them through in the end, but it was a very near thing.

Overnights were an extra attraction of Box Canyon Boys Camp. By twos the tribes went on four overnights during the summer, camping in the

Grand Canyon, in Monument Valley on the Navajo Reservation, in Oak Creek Canyon, and in the Painted Desert or Petrified Forest. One morning in the sixth week the Apaches and Bedwetters, together with their junior counselors and supervised by a senior, headed in two pickups for Havasu Canyon, a section of the Grand. Parking on the rim, they marched in single file, backpacking food, gear, and chamber pot. Down they hiked, escorted by eagles, down for two and a half hours and eight miles, the first five tortuous and steep, the last three over a lowering trail. Down, down they were let into the epochs, into deer and blinding light and fossil silences and echo. It was hot in the canyon deeps, and it was a bliss of boys to flop in cottonwood shade, then peel and plunge naked into the pool beneath Havasu Falls, to sport like otters in and through and out of mist and tumbling, shivery river. If you clambered up beside the lip of the falls and pushed off with enough force, you could arch over a rock outcrop and dive into the pool, a drop of forty terrifying feet. The Apaches did, they were older and athletic, they won at everything, and after shouts of cowardice the Bedwetters dared, all but Lally 2. When Cotton's back was turned, the Apaches lugged the youngster up, swung him by arms and legs, and let him go. His scream, as he hurtled, echoed for miles.

He screamed again in the night, waking into trauma. To comfort him, Cotton zipped his sleeping bag over his head.

It rained, too, and the tribes slept fitfully.

In the morning they explored, swam again, and after lunch made packs and filled canteens from a spring preparatory to the climb. There was a ruckus. Cocksure they'd reach the rim long before the Bedwetters, the Apaches intended, once there, to take off for camp in their pickup rather than wait for the slowpokes. But the senior counselor said to wait, he wanted the expedition back in one piece, and besides, the Bedwetters wouldn't be long after. The Apaches hooted. They offered to bet: their buffalo head, for the last two weeks of camp, against the chamber pot, that they would hit the rim a full hour faster. Cotton took it. Watches were synchronized and the party set out.

For three miles, over the easy gradient, the Bedwetters kept pace. When the true ascent began they fell back. The air, after rain, was unusually humid. Canyon walls compressed it. They sweat buckets. Lagging behind Cotton, secretly they tipped canteens. With two miles to go they were out of water. Packs galled. They commenced to throw gear away. Granite and sandstone cached heat during the day and now, like lungs, expelled it. The trail seemed to sheer straight up. A mile below the rim they heard brays of contempt. The Apaches were there, watching them, and timing. Suddenly the Bedwetters fell apart. Goodenow and Lally 2 sat down blubbering. Teft and Shecker and Lally 1 crawled into the shade of boulders and lay down wheezing. A disgusted Wheaties ordered them to haul ass, and when they wouldn't budge, went on by himself. They were alone.

*Cotton put down the pot and checked the time.
They must take the last mile in twenty-eight minutes. So he shouted at his battalion. He begged
them, but in vain. They had met only by chance.
They were joined only by jeer and neuroses and
futility. Now the delicate membrane which had held
them together in their desperation was sundered. He
was angrier with himself than with them. He had
asked more than they could give. He should never
have taken the bet. It was a command failure. And it
meant much more than handing over a damn china
crock. Lately, for the first time in their lives, they
were winning. If he let them lose now, they lost each
other. And losing each other, each one lost himself.
He saw the entire summer dangle on the side of a
damn canyon.*

*"God, you guys," he rasped, his throat scratchy,
afraid he might whimper himself. "God. You gotta
move. I still got half a canteen, you can have that."
They groaned. "Okay, I'm gonna tell you. I wasn't
but now I will. I heard the counselors talking one
night. They said we should be locked up, not sent to
a camp. They said our folks sent us here to get rid of
us and didn't know how else to unless they dumped
us out of a car or shot us." He let them think that
over. "What I'm saying is, we are dings. We're in
everybody's hair and we don't fit anywhere and
nobody wants us. Our folks, the counselors, nobody
—and most of all those loudmouths up there don't
want us up there in the next twenty-eight minutes.
Okay, we're pooped, but are we gonna let 'em piss in
our pot again? Hell we are! So move! If we don't*

now, we never will!" Tears started. Stumbling from one to the next, he kicked them frantically in the ribs. "So move, you poor bastards, you poor damn useless dings, move!"

Cotton never figured out which did it, the pain or the shame, but they did move. He passed his canteen and sent Teft to the point and took the rear and chewed them out whenever they slowed. Between them, he and Shecker dragged Lally 2 the last hundred yards. They reached the rim with four minutes to spare and dropped dead.

When he could, Cotton stood up and walked a crooked line past the counselors to the Apaches, waiting stolidly in their pickup. As soon as they hit camp, he said, his lower lip cracked and bleeding, hand over that damn buffalo head. Then he walked back to the Bedwetters and got them on their feet.

"You watch," he said. "You watch."

Taking the chamber pot by one handle, he cocked his arm, crouched, and whirling, as though he were throwing a discus, heaved it over the rim. They were free.

"Teft fired again. Out on the preserve the men leaped into their vehicles and came on.

"Hey, Teft! Clutch on the left, brake on the right—right?" Cotton was in the truck, head out the window. "So how do I shift—with this whatchy by the steering wheel? Up or down?"

20

T EFT GOGGLED.

Started in some inexpedient gear, the pickup buckjumped. Cotton floored the accelerator and the engine bellowed and they took off. Hunched over the wheel, dropped tailgate clanging, he sighted on a section of fence between two posts.

O twayne me a twim, where the ffubalo jym, where the rede and the telopen zoom; where nibber is nat, a conframitous rat-tat-tat.

He was dead on target. Impacted by grill and bumper at its center point, the taut linkage sheared with a twang and the two halves rolled back with release of tension like a curtain parted violently. The truck poured through and parked itself, since Cotton was evidently unable to locate the brake, on top of a small scrub cedar tree.

The Bedwetters might have managed a last, loco laugh except that Teft the sharpshooter fired again and hit something, because the lead jeep scurried behind a rise and Teft, tearing at the cartridge box, discovered it was empty.

The pickup spun wheels and hopscotched off the stunted tree and circled and came back through the gap like a traveling rodeo and Cotton, who must have found what clutch and brake were for, snubbed up just as Teft stood tall and grabbing the rifle by the barrel raised it over his head and chopped down and smashed the stock into splinters.

"Dings!" howled Teft. "Outa gas, outa hay, outa ammo—dings all the way!"

Cotton smiled. He never smiled. "Hell we are," he said. He lit another cigar and puffed omniscient smoke. Even in their condition they were dumbfounded. They drifted in to him like strays, hesitantly, fearful he had snapped his ultimate cap.

Except for the engine idling, it was very quiet. Cotton had a quick look at the herd, restless now as it nosed among weeds for alfalfa, then one at the pursuit. The jeep and two pickups and the men were five hundred yards away and closing fast.

Then he reviewed his regiment. Long gone and far out they might be, but at least they were not sucking thumbs or biting nails or grinding teeth. He smiled again, every sign of his seizure erased, and for a moment, inexplicably, he reminded them of an old soldier sitting on a bench by the courthouse in Prescott, recollecting his boyhood and watching the world go by and chewing on the idea of eternity.

"Hell we are," he repeated. "I'm proud of us. We said we'd finish and we are. That herd's gonna bust out and so're we. Now. For good."

Avoiding his loose tooth, he got a heroic grip on the cigar with his molars. "You watch, men," he told them around it. "You watch."

He shifted. The transmission shrieked. The truck lurched ahead. When he had steam up he transcribed a wide, slewing half-circle out on the range, the tailgate clanging like a tin can on a pup's tail, and bore down on the herd from the rear at forty mph. They saw him throw the cigar.

Fifty yards from the animals he laid on the horn. That did it.

The herd detonated. Forty-seven beasts and two calves jumped three feet straight up and hit top speed before they came down and tails high tore for the hole in the fence and boomed through it like greased lightning, boy and pickup and horn on their heels. They made a splendid thunder. It pulled down temples. It smote the ears of gnats and governments. It caused an impious planet to slip a cog. It must have been heard in heaven.

The Bedwetters saw the buffalo trophy bounce from the end of the bed. They saw the drover's head out the cab window and listened to him yahoo:

"Dings! Dings! C'mon, you dings, let's go!"

Two bulls led the breakout. Beyond the fence, pivoting at the last possible instant, at the verge of the rim, they split the herd. Half to the right, half to the left, it skedaddled off into the wide open spaces of these United States, where it belonged. But the Judas truck kept true and awful course.

Running and stumbling after it in shock, they did not know whether the brakes had failed or he had ignored them or tried to cut an ignition system which would not cut because it was double-wired or had forgotten the rim or whether he simply did not give a glorious goddam because it was gloriously finished and the buffalo were free, free, forever free, or what. They had a last glimpse of John Cotton's red hair flaming like a torch as the truck seemed to soar and dive and disappear. And that was all, except for the remote but unmistakable concussion of metal and rock and the recognition of its meaning, which, microseconds later, cracked their hearts even as it freed them, too, forever.

O twayne me a twim, where the ffubalo jym, where the rede and the telopen zoom; where nibber is nat, a conframitous rat-tat-tat, and the dils are not icky all doom.

The jeep and two pickups dusted through the break in the fence and stopped abruptly. A dozen men jumped from them, then hesitated.

The morning sun was steadfast now, the air blithe as a cool bottle of cola, and the countenance of the earth was fair. But a sad wind sneaked out of the canyon below, moaning baby, baby, and the blues and trembling through the pines and fanning over the preserve in farewell. It grieved.

Squinting under big hats, the men advanced, their faces grim. Some of them wore state uniforms. Some were sixpack city sportsmen and carried merciless rifles. Then they stopped abruptly.

Before them, standing frightened and defiant at the very jaw of the Mogollon Rim, were five redeye, hayhead juvenile delinquents in dirty boots and jeans and jackets with BC on the backs, one of them hugging the head and horns of a bull buffalo and all of them in tears. Lawrence Teft, III, and Samuel Shecker and Gerald Goodenow and Stephen Lally, Jr., and William Lally were bunched up bawling in their sorrow and jeering in their triumph over what seemed to be the sound of a radio. "Yah! Yah! Yah!" they sobbed and jeered at the men in ridiculous hats. "Yah! Yah! Yah!"

READER'S SUPPLEMENT

Bless the Beasts & Children, first published in 1970, has been a favorite young adult literary classic for generations of students. This 25th anniversary edition is being published with a reader's supplement to guide students and educators through the many themes and rich symbolism this book incorporates.

The popularity of this book among both educators and students is undoubtedly due to the emotional impact the reader gets from being able to identify with the stories of these unforgettable characters. Like other books that reach "classic" status, this book leaves an indelible mark.

Additionally, with a quarter-century span between reissues, the novel moves into the category of a "snapshot in time" that explores the American psyche of the seventies—a time of turmoil and rapid change with ramifications felt by all subsequent generations.

Historical Context: The Book and the Times

Bless the Beasts & Children is very much a story of its times. Although it was first published in 1970, the events of the book take place in the late sixties, probably in the summer of 1966. The experiences of the six boys—Cotton, Teft, Shecker, Goodenow, Lally 1 and Lally 2—are deeply embedded in the sights, sounds and atmosphere of the period. Their memories and conversations are laced with references to Vietnam, "hippies" and other expressions that belong to that decade's vocabulary. The boys see *The Professionals* at the drive-in. They discuss popular television shows. They almost always carry their transistor radios, listening to the music of Dionne Warwick, Johnny Cash, the Temptations, Jimmie Rodgers, and Gladys Knight and the Pips.

The sixties was a time of transition and turmoil, of seismic political shifts and radical changes. It was the decade that saw the Peace Corps and the Peace Movement, "Camelot" and the Counterculture, the Great Society and Vietnam, peaceful civil rights marches and violent protests against the war. By the end of it, President John F. Kennedy and one of his brothers, Senator Robert F. Kennedy, Dr. Martin Luther King and Malcolm X were all dead—assassinated—and with them, a perception of safety and permanence in our society were gone.

This is a time of transition for the boys in the story too, and it is no accident that Swarthout sets the main action near the end of a long, difficult summer. Cotton, Teft, Shecker, Goodenow and the two Lally brothers come together at the Box Canyon Boys Camp, a summer camp to which they are sent by their well-to-do but dysfunctional parents. The camp is run according to a tradition of misinterpreted western values and cruel competitiveness ("Send Us a Boy—We'll Send you a Cowboy!"). Unathletic and maladjusted, the six misfit boys are soon despised and tormented by the other campers, who label the group the "Bedwetters."

One day, on the way back from an outing, the six boys witness the government-sanctioned slaughter of buffalo on a nearby game preserve by nonprofessional hunters. The buffalo are tame and trusting; the hunters are inept. The result is bloody carnage, accomplished as easily as shooting fish in a barrel. Shocked and horrified, the Bedwetters decide to take on a heroic and dangerous mission: to release the remaining buffalo to the wild before the next day's shooting.

Acknowledging the boys' loyalty to one another and the noble idealism of their cause, Cotton, their leader, nevertheless warns them:

We think tonight's something we have to do or we wouldn't be here. But if we think it'll make us heroes or any movie junk like that, it won't. No one else will give a damn but us. In fact, it'll make a lot of people mad enough to shoot us. So what I'm saying is, it doesn't matter to anybody but us.

This note of cynicism and even despair runs throughout the book and it's no wonder. The end of the boys' adventure is also the beginning of their adult lives. The sixties are coming to a close and Watergate is just around the corner.

Nonetheless, if *Bless the Beasts & Children* is a book of its times, it is also one that transcends any time period. The questions it asks and the issues it addresses—ecology and animal rights, individualism and peer pressure, group bonding and masculine identity, the impact of media and popular mythology, and the relations between parents and children, older and younger generations—are just as pertinent and in need of exploration today. Perhaps even more so.

Discussion Questions

1. This novel was published during a period in the United States which saw the beginnings of unprecedented "grass roots" political movements for civil rights and the rights of women, gays and

the humane treatment of animals. Describe the social, political and world events of the 1960s and early 1970s in terms of each of these movements. How much progress have we made in this country since that time?

2. The experiences of Cotton and his companions are filtered through the prism of the popular media. For example, when the boys can no longer receive their radio stations, they feel "orphaned." Arizona is described as "Technicolor Country." Lally 2 remarks that when little kids see the released buffalo, "It'll be better for them than TV." Research the popular culture of the period. What were the most popular songs, television programs and movies? What messages might young people have gotten from the popular culture of the time?

3. Imagine the surviving Bedwetters alive today. How old would they be? What might their personalities and relationships be like now? Do you think they would raise their own children differently from the way they were brought up?

4. Attitudes toward the proper role of children have radically changed through time. Compare children on the farms in seventeenth-century colonial America, those working in factories during the Industrial Revolution and children today. Overall, have the lives of children become better or worse during the past three centuries?

Narrative: The Author and His Style

A number of media theorists have noted the similarities between novels and film. Although one is a print medium and the other is visual, both offer linear narratives dependent upon plot, setting, characterization and dialogue. Sometimes they even mimic each other's storytelling techniques. For example, the beginning of Charles Dickens's *A Tale of Two Cities* ("It was the best of times, it was the worst of times . . .") is reminiscent of montage, a form of film editing in which a great deal of information is supplied in a short period of time.

Author Glendon Swarthout's talent for creating richly detailed settings and vivid characters through physical detail seems highly cinematic—that is, you can almost "see" the individual boys and the Arizona landscape through which they travel.

This cinematic quality is particularly evident in the book's structure, which mimics another film technique—flashback. Like *Jason and the Golden Fleece, Don Quixote* and the stories of King Arthur's search for the Holy Grail, *Bless the Beasts & Children* is a quest plot. As Ronald B. Tobias points out in his book, *Twenty Master Plots and How to Build Them* (1993), in this form of story, the object of the search is everything to the protagonists involved. The act of questing and the ultimate outcome of the quest will change them forever.

Of course, to understand how the Bedwetters are being transformed by their self-appointed mission to save the buffalo, we must know something about what they were like before. And so, the story "flashes back" at appropriate points in the quest narrative, offering us bits and pieces of the boys' pasts spent in the camp and with their families. The effect is somewhat like assembling a jigsaw puzzle, and by the end we have all the information we need to see the big picture.

Swarthout works hard to delineate one boy from another, marking each as an individual. In addition to the usual physical descriptions (Cotton is a redhead; Teft is tall; Shecker, overweight, etc.) each boy adopts a distinctive headgear that also serves as a symbol for his internal state. The boys all have individual problems but they discover that they have individual strengths too. For example, Cotton may be the leader, but it is Shecker who is strong enough to break open the bale of hay and Teft who is experienced enough to drive the truck.

Bless the Beasts & Children also evokes an acute sense of place. All the cities and towns that the boys travel through on their journey are carefully and lovingly depicted, from Montezuma Street in downtown Prescott, past the abandoned mines of Mingus Mountain, along Route 66 to the treacherous beauty of the Mogollon Rim.

In addition to its film-like qualities, the book offers pleasures that only a book can: creative word-play and thought-provoking metaphors. Swarthout is ingenious and imaginative in his use of words, whether he is describing Teft ("a tilted boy who walked around with a tilted smile") or a herd of buffalo ("plodding its patient way to a frontier not yet found, snorting clouds and bumping heavens with its humps and hooking stars with its horns").

The boys don't just crawl into sleeping bags but "seal themselves into envelopes of down and wool and nylon." When they are afraid, "anxieties like mosquitoes beset them." One boy "periscopes" his head; another flicks away "an onion tear." Air feels cool like a bottle of cola. The sun "chins" the horizon. Such passages engage and absorb the reader, sending an occasional shiver of recognition up the spine.

Discussion Questions

1. Swarthout uses flashbacks extensively to flesh out his characters' lives. Is this an effective technique? What effect does this have on the reader's understanding of the story? How does this presentation preclude the reader from prejudging each character?

2. Using atlases and road maps, trace the boys' journey from the camp to the Mogollon Rim. Research the locations they pass through in the

state of Arizona. Has the author captured the look and feel of the places accurately?

3. Reread the story, noting words, expressions and metaphors that you find interesting or unusual. How do these passages add to the enjoyment of the story?

4. Write a character sketch for each boy, noting his physical appearance, his headgear, his skills and weaknesses and his personal habits. Do these boys seem like real people you've known or might know? Contrast them with the other boys in the camp. Were Cotton and his friends truly "misfits"?

5. *Bless the Beasts & Children* has much in common with other books about troubled adolescents. Compare the handling of similar themes found in other stories, such as William Golding's *Lord of the Flies* (violence and peer pressure), John Knowles's *A Separate Peace* (friendship) and J.D. Salinger's *Catcher in the Rye* (alienation), and in films, such as *Stand by Me* (male bonding) and *The Wizard of Oz* (the quest).

Ethical Questions: Boys and Buffaloes

The central theme of the novel, of course, is contained in the title. What *Bless the Beasts & Children* is most concerned about is how society treats our most innocent and defenseless creatures: animals and children. It is one of the first books of its kind to explore two important issues of our modern society: animal rights and throwaway children.

Parallels between the boys and the buffalo are repeatedly drawn throughout the book. Wheaties, the boys' counselor at the camp, calls his charges "dings":

A ding, he said, was something or somebody which didn't fit anything or anywhere. It used up space but it was useless. Nobody wanted it or knew what to do with it. Therefore it had no excuse for being or living.

The same might be said of the buffalo herds that roam the preserve. No longer needed to feed cattle and clothe the Native American tribes of the Plains, the buffalo have outgrown what society perceives as their "usefulness." No one knows what to do with them and so they are physically enclosed and restricted and eventually "thinned" out in a biennial government-sanctioned event that allows tourists to take easy shots at the buffalo for sport and entertainment.

Witnessing the cruel, physically abusive slaughter of the buffalo, the boys are instinctually empathetic. They, too, have been abused. The parents we glimpse in the flashbacks seem to be the very epitome of "toxic parents": immature, self-absorbed, controlling, neglectful, verbally and physically abusive. As a result of the poisonous family relationships, all of the boys feel deep shame about themselves, a feeling which the noted author John Bradshaw calls "soul murder," the total denial of self.

Box Canyon Boys Camp, where the six protagonists have been sent by their parents for the summer, adopts a social hierarchy system based on an internal code of success, enforced by peer pressure and established through athletic ability. It is run according to rules that are a twisted perception of masculine values. Competition is not only encouraged but enforced with cruel, humiliating punishments for those who can't or won't "play the game." Interestingly, the system is also set up to reward cheating ("Raiding was good for the boys. It taught grit. Into character it built cunning . . ."), so long as the efforts were successful. The message is clear: win at all costs.

All boys require an initiation, a rite of passage, say theorists on masculinity, but rituals that "make a man out of you" through cruelty and humiliation create only a twisted, stunted and false sense of manhood. Faced with ineffective initiation rites, adolescent boys will create their own, and that's exactly what Cotton and his companions do. Saving the buffalo becomes their rite of passage into maturity.

Swarthout emphasizes the contrast between the boy's cooperative, caring, nonviolent act with the violence of the buffalo killers. Note, too, that these killers, or "shooters," are not stereotypical male hunters, but a young woman, an elderly physician and a teenage boy. By presenting us with these average people caught up in the bloodlusting, carnival atmosphere of the shoot ("Children romped about to glean the bullet casings . . ."), the author indicts our entire society. Within this culture of violence, he is saying, is it any wonder that the beasts and the children are at risk?

Discussion Questions

1. Discuss the rules and traditions of the Box Canyon Boys Camp. What sort of ethical structure provides the foundation for such a system? How is the campers' drive for "success at all costs" at odds with the American work ethic and our traditional values of honesty, loyalty and living by "the Golden Rule"?

2. Chapter 11 lies at the thematic heart of the story. Reread this chapter, paying close attention to the last few paragraphs. Was it possible for the buffalo to be managed more humanely? What are the ethical considerations in using animals to benefit humans? What is the author saying about endangered species like the buffalo, the endangerment of our children and the status of "the American soul"?

3. Locate all the passages in the book that link the boys with the buffalo. Is the boys' situation comparable to the plight of the buffalo? If so, how? How do the boys and the buffalo come to understand one another? Why does Lally 2 seem to have the closest relationship with the animals in the book, first with his horse and, later, with the buffalo?

4. Research theories on masculinity found in the works of poet Robert Bly, writer Sam Keen and others. What do they mean when they say a boy must "become" a man? What is the definition of masculinity in our society? In the final analysis, who was more "masculine"—the Bedwetters or the other boys at the camp? Is there a comparable code of femininity for women? How has it changed in the decades since this book was written?

5. Describe the bonding experience between the boys. Why did they "bump" and how did it reinforce their friendship?

Symbolism: Sagebrush and Saviors

With the exception of the younger Lally brother, whose special relationship with his horse, Sheba, helps him win the barrel race, none of the Bedwetters seems to be especially proficient at learning the cowboy skills taught at the camp.

Nevertheless, the group (and Cotton in particular) find the *image* of the cowboy enormously appealing.

In his famous essay "The Westerner," Robert Warshow describes the classic film cowboy as "a figure in repose," a simple man, a man of leisure— lonely, melancholic, not especially talkative and not too concerned with material possessions other than his horse and gun. In the classic cinema western "where men are men," it is always 1870, just after the Civil War.

Throughout *Bless the Beasts & Children* the six protagonists compare themselves, their world and, ultimately, their mission to the cowboy ideal they've seen in the 1966 film *The Professionals*. Ironically, *The Professionals* is not an ideal classic western at all. It belongs to that category of popular films produced in the sixties and seventies that came to be known as "anti-westerns" or "new" westerns.

Unlike the John Wayne/John Ford type of classic western, anti-westerns are usually set after the turn of the century. Rather than optimistic, they are cynical. Their heroes aren't noble men in white hats but misfits and scoundrels motivated by the need for adventure or money. The world of the anti-western is a corrupt and treacherous place, unprotective of the helpless and innocent. The Indians are all but gone, the bankers and railroad tycoons are in charge. Heroes of anti-westerns, who are not loners but usually part of a group, depend on their own luck, grit and determination and upon each other. Codes of ethics were usually made up as they went along.

Cotton and his friends, of course, don't understand the distinction between classic and anti-westerns, but Swarthout, who went on to write *The Shootist,* does. It seems highly appropriate that the Bedwetters should choose as their model *The Professionals,* which is the story of four tough misfit loners with distinctly individual skills who cross a no-man's land of desert to accomplish an ill-fated rescue mission. The film is, as Swarthout describes it, "a yarn innocent and scabrous, brutal and principled, true and a liar," but the literal story isn't as important as the spirit the boys internalize from it. Swarthout observes, "You did not watch it. You sucked on it."

On the other hand, there has always been a relationship between the western mystique and religious imagery, as Michael Marsden notes in his essay "Savior in the Saddle: the Sagebrush Testament." Shane, Gary Cooper's sheriff in *High Noon,* the gunfighters of *The Magnificent Seven,* even the pragmatic rescuers of *The Professionals* are all "saviors" of one kind or another, so it is no surprise that *Bless the Beasts & Children* is rich in religious symbolism. The American West is likened to the Canaan of the Chosen People. The meeting of boys and buffalo is reminiscent of Adam's mingling with animals in the Garden of Eden.

In addition, just as the boys act as savior to the

buffalo, so John Cotton saves the boys from their pasts, guiding them into maturity. Is it a coincidence that his initials are "JC," or that the boys interpret the camp initials on their jackets as "Before Christ"? Cotton's commanding, paternal attitude toward his companions, the whiskey "sacrament" and, finally, the "betrayal" of the Judas truck leading to Cotton's death all reinforce the character's Christ-like persona.

Discussion Questions

1. Discuss the similarities between John Cotton and Jesus Christ. How many can you find? Compare Cotton to savior figures in other stories, such as McMurphy in Ken Kesey's *One Flew Over the Cuckoo's Nest*. What do these characters have in common?

2. Watch films like *The Magnificent Seven, The Wild Bunch, Butch Cassidy and the Sundance Kid* and other anti-westerns from the '60s and '70s. What elements do they have in common? How do they compare to classic westerns like *Shane* and *Stagecoach*?

3. In addition to the cowboy references, *Bless the Beast & Children* also contains many allusions to Native American culture. How does the camp use—or misuse—this culture for its own pur-

poses? Describe Shecker's buffalo dance and discuss what it means.

4. The book often juxtaposes the romantic myth of the Old West and the present-day reality of the contemporary West. How do the two compare? Which do you think the author prefers?

5. All the boys at the camp imagine themselves in terms of the cowboy mythos. Who do you think are better cowboys, the Bedwetters or the other campers?

About the Author of the Reader's Supplement

C. W. Walker is an award-winning journalist, film critic and writer on popular culture. She has taught courses in film, screenwriting and journalism at the New School for Social Research in New York City, and at Jersey City State College and Rutgers University in New Jersey. She is a doctoral candidate at the School of Communication, Information and Library Science at Rutgers University.